I0689754

GHOST TOWNIES BOOK ONE
GHOSTRIDDEN
E.J. RUSSELL

Cover design: L.C. Chase, http://lcchase.com
Cover model: Nicholas Katen, photographed by Sam San Román
Edited by Meg DesCamp

ISBN: 978-1-947033-99-3

First edition
August 2024

Contact information:
ejr@ejrussell.com

GHOST TOWNIES BOOK ONE
GHOSTRIDDEN
E.J. RUSSELL

CHAPTER ONE

"Holy crap, Gil. I never expected *this*."

Gilgamesh, predictably, didn't answer, not even a meow or the weird yodeling yowl he'd been favoring me with for most of the three-hour-plus drive from Portland. Maybe he was just happy the car had stopped moving. For that matter, so was I. But seriously?

"There's got to be some mistake."

I wrestled the cranky door of my rattletrap Civic open and clambered out onto the street to gawk. When the probate lawyer with the awesome double-barreled name of Taryn Pasternak-McHale had called to tell me I'd inherited a house from my Uncle Oren, my first response had been, "Uncle who?"

I'd had no idea I even *had* an Uncle Oren, and technically, I still didn't, him being dead and all. But even when he was alive, the relationship had been distant at best: He was apparently my mother's second cousin once removed, and I defy anybody who's not a total genealogy geek to figure that one out. But Taryn-with-the-great-name had assured me that I was right there in the will.

"We've had a terrible time finding you," she'd said, her voice over the phone line noticeably irritable. "It took us two months. We had to hire a private detective."

I winced. "Sorry." Yeah, couch surfing didn't exactly give you a fixed address to use for mail forwarding, and I'd scaled back my online presence after I'd gotten trolled multiple times thanks to my vindictive ex. Speaking of whom… "Did you try leaving a message with Greg Findler? He's still at my last permanent address."

"Several times." She cleared her throat. "He, ah, told us you were dead."

"What?"

"To be fair, he amended the statement to say you were dead to *him*, but he was less than helpful."

"I can believe that," I muttered. "So how did you find me?"

"You were listed as the 'with' author on Dale Usher's memoir. We tracked you through his publisher."

"Ah." Most of the time, ghostwriting didn't get you a by-line or even a mention in the acknowledgements. Dale, a retired detective with a strong commitment to justice and fair play, had been an exception. In fact, he'd insisted on giving me credit, both on the cover and in his comments. "Good to know."

Taryn rattled off a bunch of details. To be honest, I didn't hear half of what she said because my head was still reeling from the double shock that I'd had a relative I hadn't known about, and that he'd left me a freaking *house*, for Pete's sake.

Okay, triple shock: that Greg was still pissed enough at me for refusing to ghostwrite *his* book that he wasn't satisfied with trashing my professional rep online, but was refusing to pass on messages, even though I checked with him daily via text.

His response was always, *"No messages, no mail, screw you."*

"The house is a bit remote," Taryn warned. "In a small town between Eugene and Florence."

Considering all my Portland bridges had been torched very merrily by Greg, I'd said, "Sounds perfect," arranged for her to message the key and directions to me at the nearest UPS store, and hit the road immediately to the not-so-musical accompaniment of Gil's very vocal disapprobation.

With nothing else to distract me on the drive—my phone died outside Eugene and the Civic's radio hadn't worked since 2013—I'd tried to imagine what kind of house my uncle had left me. I'd run the gamut from a two-room shack to a 50s ranch to a mossy log cabin with a crooked smoke pipe to a creepy Victorian that would give the Bates Motel a run for its money. I'd never come close to *this*.

My incomplete degrees in English lit, creative writing, and business didn't qualify me as an architectural expert, but I knew Queen Anne when I saw it because I'd researched it for a ghostwriting gig for a historical romance author.

Uncle Oren's house—*my* house—was a classic example, including the steep, asymmetrical roof, the cross gables, the polygonal tower at one side of the full-width front porch, and all the decorative goodies on shingles and woodwork and trim and just *everywhere*.

As for being dilapidated, creepy, or even in need of a new coat of paint? Nope, nope, and nope. It was absolutely pristine. Even the round stained glass window in the third floor gable gleamed in the April sunlight.

My embarrassing schoolkid squeal was masked by the usual *screech* of metal as I closed the Civic's door. With my wide, manic grin, I probably resembled a deranged clown, but I couldn't help it.

Besides, there was nobody to see. My house—*my house!*—was flanked at a considerable distance by two others, one a yellow rambling two-story farmhouse style, and the other a brown and green craftsman bungalow. We were the only houses on the quiet, one-block street; a park populated by enormous trees and surrounded by a tall wrought-iron fence lay opposite.

I practically skipped around the car to grapple Gil's carrier out of the passenger seat. "Come on, buddy. Let's see what our *new home* is like."

As anxious as I was to see if the inside matched the outside, I didn't rush to the front door—I was too busy rubbernecking. I'd have thought that since Taryn hadn't been able to reach me for two months—yeah, thanks for that, Greg—that the landscaping would have gotten a little ragged at least, but my front yard was as manicured as both my neighbors'. A huge maple stood halfway between the street and the house, its branches canopying a curved flagstone walk lined with nodding purple pansies. The path was bordered by smooth swaths of green lawn without a single invading dandelion in sight.

Maybe the neighbors had banded together to keep it looking nice so their own places didn't lose curb appeal? Or maybe the upkeep had been included in Uncle Oren's bequest, one of the details I'd missed as I'd tried not to pass out from shock over owning a freaking *house*.

I mounted the porch steps and set Gil's carrier down on the wide, whitewashed planks of its deck. "It has a porch swing, Gil!" I may have squealed again, but can you blame me? An actual porch swing! I couldn't believe my impossibly good luck.

I dug the key out of my rear jeans pocket. It had poked me in the butt all the way from Portland, but I endured the discomfort because it reminded me I was heading to *my house*.

I gazed fondly at its funky keychain: the Scooby Gang, complete with psychedelic van. I counted it a point in Taryn's favor, if she was leaning in to the town's name: Ghost.

Yep, I was moving to Ghost, Oregon, and given my profession, the irony was not lost on me, especially since I hadn't had a paying gig since Greg started his online flame campaign.

The dark wooden front door was rounded on the top, with a leaded half-moon light at eye level. I didn't peek through, though, any more than I peered through the windows that fronted the porch, because I wanted my first step across the threshold to rival the final reveal in all those house-flipping DIY shows.

That I may watch. Or binge. A lot. Hey, it's for *research*.

I poised the key over the lock. "Here goes, Gil." But when I tried to insert it into the keyhole? No dice. I couldn't even get the tip inside.

Okay, now *this* was more like my luck, not to mention my love life. I owned a house, but I couldn't get inside. I narrowed my eyes at the gleaming brass lock collar. "Not very welcoming, house. We need to have a little chat."

I crouched down to peer into the keyhole. Something was definitely jammed inside. It was stuffed full of something that looked like—

"You there! You on the porch! Back away. Now."

Chapter Two

I froze in my crouch, but lifted my arms *slooowly* to the side, keeping my hands in full view. I'd had enough experience getting pulled out of line for extra scanning at airports to know a guy who looked like me, with my obvious Middle Eastern features and shoulder-length mop of black hair, shouldn't make any sudden moves around skittish people who may or may not be carrying weapons.

"I'm standing up now," I called.

"Drop whatever you've got in your hand. I've got pepper spray and a Taser, and I'm not afraid to use either one of them."

Well, at least he didn't have a gun. Unless he was saving that for later.

"It's only my keys." But I dropped them anyway. "I'm turning around now." Because, yeah, I'd rather not get tased in the back, and although the pepper spray might be an issue, no way was I *not* looking this person in the eye. So I turned slowly, edging sideways as I did to block Gil's carrier.

The guy at the foot of the sidewalk was about my age—late twenties, maybe early thirties—and good-looking in a sleek, expensive way that I'd never manage on my best day. One of those haircuts brushed back smoothly on the top, that only worked if you had straight hair and not corkscrew curls like me. He was wearing jeans, but they were clearly much newer than my faded 501's, his loafers were shiny, and his button-down had nary a wrinkle. The contrast to my battered Converse and sweaty PSU T-shirt couldn't be greater.

With his phone in one hand and the other digging in the leather messenger bag slung across his shoulder, he was obviously taking me in too, eyes narrowed in his clean-shaven face. Also obviously, he wasn't impressed.

"You have three minutes to vacate the premises before I call the police."

I pasted on a smile. "It's okay. I'm supposed to be here."

"I doubt that seriously. The house belongs to—"

"Me." I shrugged apologetically, hands still in the air. "The house belongs to me."

His square jaw sagged. "You?"

"Afraid so."

"But... But..." He took a step toward me. "What's your name?"

"Maz. Mazin Amani."

He blinked. "Armani?"

"Not *Ar*mani. *A*mani." Given his trendy clothing, I guessed that the missing R would have made a difference to him. "I inherited this house from my Uncle Oren." Well, second cousin once removed Oren, but even though I'd never known he existed, let alone met him, I wasn't about to look a gift house in the mouth. Er, porch. "And you are?"

He blinked again. "Oren Buckley was your uncle? I had no idea..." He withdrew his hand—thankfully Taser and pepper-spray free—from his bag and tucked his phone in his pocket as he strode up the sidewalk toward me. "I'm so sorry. I'm Carson Clemenson. Avi's cousin."

It was my turn to blink. "Avi?"

"Avi Felder." His eyebrows drew together. "Surely you knew about Avi."

"Sorry." I wiped my hands on my jeans. "I never even knew I had an Uncle Oren until the probate attorney called me."

"Avi and Oren were..." He sighed. "Well, if Avi hadn't died before the US passed marriage equality, I'm pretty sure they'd have been husbands. They were devoted to one another." The guy's eyes swam with unshed tears. He coughed out a half laugh. "Sorry. Avi and I were close. I still miss him." He gazed up at the house. "We had some times in this place."

At my feet, Gil made his opinion known with a snarly yowl. I winced.

"I'm sorry for your loss, but it's been a long trip, and Gilgamesh really wants his dinner. So if you don't mind?" I gestured toward the door.

"Oh. Of course." He screwed his mouth to one side, which didn't mar the perfect symmetry of his face as much as you'd think. "I'm afraid it could be a bit of a mess. Nobody's been inside since Avi's death."

I raised my eyebrows. "Really?" Not even second cousin once removed Oren? I glanced around the perfectly maintained yard and the pristine paint and woodwork. *Somebody* must have cared for it. "It looks incredible."

"Yes, out here." He nodded toward the house next door. "The same person who handles the neighbor's upkeep has been maintaining the exterior."

"For over ten years?"

The attorney hadn't mentioned any ongoing expenses attached to the estate. Surely, if someone had been doing this much work for a decade, there should have been mention of it. But then, she'd also told me that there were boxes of Uncle Oren's effects in storage that would be shipped to me here. Maybe the records for the handyman's payments were in them.

"It's been a couple of months since Uncle Oren died. I hope his bill isn't too much past due."

"Oh, I don't think he's paid for the work."

It was my turn to goggle. "Not paid? But clearly—"

"I don't know anything for certain. But the guy worked for Oren and Avi when they both lived here, from the time he was a teenager. Maybe there was some provision." His expression darkened. "Or maybe he thought Oren would leave the place to him if he kept it up."

"Uh…"

Carson showed his palms and chuckled. "Oh, not that I think there's anything nefarious going on. But people get funny when money and property are involved. I'm a real estate agent. Trust me. I know all about that."

I glanced at the house. "If nobody's been inside for a decade…"

I shuddered to think what the interior might be like. Spiders. Mice. Rats. *Gah*! Taryn said she'd have the utilities turned on. But what would the inside of a refrigerator that hadn't been opened in a decade smell like?

I added new appliances to my mental list of *More Things On Which to Spend Money I Don't Have.*

This inheritance had come through in the nick of time, though, so maybe I'd get lucky again. Maybe Uncle Oren—or his apparent boyfriend—had just upgraded the entire house. Heck, ten-year-old technology was practically *Star Trek* compared to what I was used to. Before I'd moved into Greg's condo six months ago, I'd lived in a seventies-era apartment with orange shag carpeting, and I still drove an '81 Civic hatchback.

But unless I could actually *get into* the house, I'd never know about the conditions inside, and I'd probably be sleeping in the back of said hatchback, because the town of Ghost—and seriously, who named their town Ghost?—was noticeably lacking in reasonably priced motels. Or any motels, for that matter.

I peered at the keyhole again. It looked like it was jammed full of… sawdust?

"Seems this lock is non-functional." I dangled the key chain—which contained a single key—and gave Carson my best smile. "I don't suppose you know any other way in, from your days here in your youth?" His brow wrinkled and his lips thinned. *Ooops*. "Not that you're not youthful now. I mean, all kids know the secret ways into and out of the house, right? How else could you sneak out when you're supposed to be doing homework?"

His expression cleared a little, but still held a shadow of disapproval. "The back door is keyed the same as the front. But other than the windows—which you'd have to break to get in—the basement bulkhead doors are the only other means of egress, and they're bolted from the inside."

I eyed the windows—beautiful double-hung panes with the wavery reflection that denoted vintage glass which, if not downright irreplaceable, would be *very* expensive to repair. Besides, it was way too soon to start breaking things—this might legally be my house, but until I released Gil to prowl the place, it wouldn't seem like I'd taken full possession.

"Back door, huh?"

He nodded, checking his watch. "Yes. I'm sorry, but I have an appointment at two and it'll take me twenty minutes to get to my office in Richdale." He pulled a business card from his shirt pocket. "Here. Feel free to give me a call if you have any questions. Maybe we can grab a cup of coffee sometime. There aren't many options for that in Ghost, but Richdale is a college town." He flashed his own smile, which I had to admit was damned attractive. "The students would riot without a reasonable assortment of coffee shops and cafes."

"Thanks." He was pinging my gaydar like crazy, but his brand of good looks screamed *high maintenance* and was way out of my league. But hey. New house, new town, why not a new me who wasn't so quick to judge? "I might take you up on that."

"I hope you do." He backed up a couple of steps and lifted a hand. "Nice to meet you, Maz. Welcome to Ghost."

He strode down the sidewalk and tossed his bag inside a shiny silver— Wait. Was that a freaking Porsche?

Yep, *way* out of my league.

I peered into Gil's carrier, but he was favoring me with his furry butt, the end of his tail twitching in full-on kitty diva mode.

"Not much longer, Gil. I promise."

I hefted his carrier, trotted down the porch steps and around the side of the house. No fence, not even of the traditional white picket variety that kept nothing in or out, including nosy neighbors.

Speaking of which…

As I passed a neatly trimmed hydrangea bush, its purple flowers a nice contrast to my house's—*my house!*—dove-gray paint, I caught a glimpse of a pale face and the glint of glasses behind the window of the bungalow next door. I raised my hand in greeting, but the curtains twitched and the face disappeared.

I sighed, wondering when the police would show up and assume, like Carson had, that someone who looked like me couldn't possibly be up to any good.

On the other hand, the homes here along Iris Lane weren't jammed together like they were in Portland or its suburbs. Maybe I'd imagined the face.

I chuckled. "Heck, Gil, maybe it was a ghost."

CHAPTER THREE

I whistled when I stepped past the corner of the house into the backyard. The place was *vast*. Okay, so vast by my city-boy terms. Maybe it wasn't the size of a football field, but it was close, and had nothing to separate it from the lawns on either side, which made it look even bigger. The grass was smooth and green across all three, the trees neatly pruned, and the flower beds tidy and colorful. The house on the other side—the yellow one—had a lush, fenced-in vegetable garden with a jaunty scarecrow on guard in its center.

I peered at the scarecrow more closely. Its outfit bore a striking resemblance to Carson's, and instead of the traditional floppy straw hat, it sported a headful of golden brown yarn smoothed over its burlap scalp.

I grinned. You had to love someone who wasn't afraid to add a little social snark to their pest control. Not everyone could have a Gilgamesh to handle that for them. The snark or the pests.

Unlike the front, the back porch wasn't the full width of the house—the basement bulkhead doors prevented it—but it was still deep and pleasant. It would be a great place to sit in the evening, watching the crows get intimidated by Carson's effigy.

I checked the steps as I mounted them. No splinters in the rails, no rot in the wood. Yeah, somebody had taken excellent care of the outside of this house, despite it standing empty for so long.

Before I tried the lock, I closed my eyes and offered up a brief plea to the universe. *Please don't be jammed. Please don't be jammed.* I squatted down and squinted at the keyhole in the shadow of the porch roof.

Crap. Apparently the universe was bent on having a laugh at my expense. I leaned my head against the door, shoulders sagging. "I don't believe it."

"Hola!"

I glanced up at the cheerful greeting. The call had come from the yellow house. A tiny woman with a crown of silver braids and a smile adding to the creases in her round face waved at me from her own back porch.

I waved back. "Hi. I'm your new neighbor." I jerked my thumb at the door. "Or will be once I can get inside. Do you happen to know if there's a locksmith in town?"

She spread her hands, palms up. "Not in this place. Not anymore. Nearest one is in Richdale. Those college students are always locking themselves out of their rooms."

I sighed and trudged down the steps. "Great. I guess I'd better give them a call."

She chuckled. "You don't need them. My godson will help you."

"Your godson? Is he a locksmith?"

"No. But he will help you, anyway." She pulled a cell phone out of her apron pocket and made a call, speaking in rapid Spanish. Then she smiled at me. "He's on his way."

"I don't want to be a bother—"

"It is no bother. He's a good boy." She gestured to her garden, the sweep of her arm encompassing my yard as well. "He takes good care of everything here."

"Wow." If her godson was responsible for the pristine state of my house—*my house!*—and yard, the guy must be a magician. Or maybe a time traveler, if he could keep all this in order as well as come whenever his godmother called him. "He does an amazing job."

She beamed. "He does. Of course, my grandson would help too, but he's away at school. Harvard!" Her smile grew even wider, obvious pride lifting her shoulders. "He graduates next month. And then he's going to law school!"

"That's great." Maybe my tone wasn't as upbeat as it could have been, but since the closest I'd ever come to an Ivy League school was ghostwriting an admissions essay for a kid who wanted to go to Dartmouth because he'd heard it was a great party school, I couldn't muster up a lot of enthusiasm.

"The first in my family to go to college. He's so *inteligente*."

"Guess he'd have to be, going to Harvard and law school and all."

She descended from her porch and walked toward me. She was probably about a foot shorter than my six-two, with the comfortably padded frame that, along with her smile, made you want to give her a hug.

"He works so hard, studying. He's made the dean's list every semester." She sighed contentedly. "I wish I could go to his graduation, but"—she spread her hands—"tuition was expensive."

I blinked at her. "You paid for him to go to Harvard?"

She cocked her head, her dark eyes as bright as a bird's. "What else is money for but to help family?"

I wouldn't know. My own folks hadn't had much, since my dad had left Syria as a virtual refugee and my mom was from midwestern farmer rootstock. They'd left enough to cover their funerals, but not much else other than memories of a happy childhood.

Which not everyone could claim, so I shouldn't complain.

"That's very generous of you."

She waved my words away. "Bah. I'm his *abuela*. What else would I do with the money? My house is my own. I have all that I need." She leaned down to peer into Gil's carrier. "Who is this handsome *gatito*?"

Gatito? I knew enough Spanish to know that meant little cat. Gil had never qualified as a *gatito*. He'd been a bruiser even as a kitten. "This is Gilgamesh. Gil." When she extended a finger toward the mesh door, I put up a hand. "Careful. He can be skittish"—read homicidal—"with strangers, and he's pretty grumpy after a long car ride."

"He wouldn't hurt me. Not such a lovely boy." She held her finger close enough to the grill that Gil would be able to swipe it with a ginger paw with no trouble, but instead, he poked his nose out and dabbed at her fingertip. And purred.

Well, I'll be damned.

"Either you have a magic touch, or he's trying to ingratiate himself with our new neighbors."

A warm chuckle sounded from behind me. "Tia Sofia can charm the birds from the trees."

"Enrique!" she chided. "Don't tease. This is our new neighbor." She stood, brushed her hands down her apron, and then patted her braids. "His *gatito* is named Gilgamesh, but he hasn't told me his own name yet."

I slapped my forehead. "D'oh! Sorry." I took a step backward so I could turn halfway to take in the new arrival as well as Sofia. "I'm…" My mouth dried and I couldn't seem to force my own name past my lips.

Because the man gazing at me with his godmother's round face and sunny smile was just about the cutest guy I'd ever seen. Not classically handsome—that would be Carson, in the non-scarecrow flesh—or what the club boys would call gorgeous, but just so… *appealing*.

Maybe it was his lovely skin, a couple of shades darker than mine turned when I managed to get more than a minute or two of sun. Maybe it was the way his shiny black hair fell over his wide forehead. Maybe it was the way his deep brown eyes crinkled at the corners with that killer smile.

Or maybe it was the friendliness that practically radiated from him, just as it did from his godmother.

You *could charm me out of anything, including my pants.*

But given my track record lately, I reminded myself sternly that I could look but not touch. Other than to shake hands, of course, because that was totally legit.

He shifted an enormous toolbox from his right hand to his left and took my offered hand, the calluses on his palm a nice abrasion against my more boring one.

Yes, I said boring, and I meant boring. Spending all your time pounding a keyboard doesn't create fascinating, idiosyncratic landmarks on your skin like other types of work, but I could appreciate friction when it presented itself.

Enrique lifted one eyebrow. "You are…?"

I closed my mouth, teeth clicking. "Right. Sorry. I'm Maz. Amani. Maz Amani."

"Nice to meet you, Maz Amani. You can call me Ricky." He turned to his godmother. "Tia, you haven't been in the garden again, have you?"

She batted at his very nice biceps. "What do I have a garden for if not to go in?"

"You have a garden so your nephew can take care of it for you. A stroll, nothing more. And did you take your pills this morning?"

She frowned at him, but it was obviously not a serious frown. Not like the kind Greg could scare up for nothing more than a misplaced throw pillow or the wrong brand of merlot.

"Yes, but doctors don't know everything. A little time in my garden will do me more good than all the pills in the world."

"Tia," he said, lowering his chin to give her a stern look. "You mustn't overdo it."

"I'm not. I'm not, I promise." Her smile dawned again. "I have to be well when Guillermo comes home this summer."

I thought I caught a shadow chasing across Enrique's—*Ricky's*—face, but figured I must be mistaken because his grin followed so quickly. "Exactly."

"I'll bring you boys some iced tea, and a little treat for the *gatito*." She bustled away toward her house.

Ricky shook his head. "She takes care of everybody except herself."

"She said you're her godson? But you said nephew…" I lifted my eyebrows. Hey, I was fishing, but I liked to get my facts straight. Nothing's more embarrassing in ghostwriting than a research error.

"Both, actually, but the godson part came first, and that ranks higher in Tia's eyes. Now." He turned the full force of his gaze on me and I might have zoned out for an instant. "Tia said you have a problem with your locks?"

I swallowed thickly, trying to bring my brain back online. "Yeah." I gestured with the Scooby keychain. "The locks seem like they're jammed with something. Looks like sawdust maybe?"

"Let's have a look then."

He climbed the steps, and yeah, I watched his ass. Because it was very nicely outlined by his untrendy Wranglers, and exactly the kind I liked—not tight and gym-toned, but still rounded and grabbable.

If, you know, I was inclined to do anything like that without the grab-ee's consent, especially after knowing him for all of two minutes, which I definitely was not.

He hunkered down and peered into the keyhole. "Just as I thought. Mason bees."

"Mason bees?"

"Yep. They're the primary pollinators around here, especially in early spring, now that the wild honeybee population is pretty much gone. They seek out protected holes like this to lay their eggs in."

I gulped. "So are we killing the primary pollinators?"

He glanced up at me, humor glinting in his eyes. "They've already hatched. This is the detritus they leave behind. They get the front door too?" I nodded. "Okay. I'll take care of this one, then clear the other while you go inside." His smile turned a little crooked. "I guess you'd like to see what your new house is like."

My brows drew together. "You know this is my new house?"

He shrugged and then turned back to the keyhole, a long tool with an odd scooped end in his hand. "Taryn's a friend. We both grew up in Ghost. She told me she'd found Oren's beneficiary, but no details, so don't worry about a lawyer-client confidentiality breach."

"I don't. Didn't. Won't."

"Glad to hear it." He finished poking in the lock and pulled what turned out to be a tiny vacuum out of his toolbox, judging from the mini-whirring of its little motor. "There." He stood up. "I could test it, but I imagine you'd rather do the honors yourself."

I confess, my throat got a little thick, and I had to swallow a couple of times, because Ricky was empathetic enough to understand what this moment meant to me.

I approached, Scooby in my hand. The key went in easily and though it didn't turn smoothly, it did turn. I opened the door.

And stepped inside *my house* for the first time.

Chapter Four

"It's okay to breathe, you know," Ricky murmured.

Because, yeah, I was holding my breath, so I let it out in a rush.

I was standing in what was apparently a slate-tiled mud room, and it had more doors than walls. The one to the right probably led to the garage I'd passed on the way to the backyard. The swinging door midway down the left wall clearly led further into the house, since, you know, that's where the rest of the house was.

The left-hand door immediately to the left was ajar, revealing a… what did they call them when a bathroom only had a sink and toilet? Powder room? Half-bath? I should know this stuff—I'd ghostwritten enough real estate copy, but for some reason, I couldn't dredge up any of it from long-term memory.

Straight ahead, almost flush with the right-hand wall, an open door revealed a landing with stairs leading both up and down. To the left of it, the walls sported shelving at my head height and again about even with my shins.

Ricky's breath hitched, and I glanced at him in concern. His eyes just cleared my shoulder and his gaze was fixed on a red fleece jacket that was hanging from one of the row of brass hooks that lined the wall under the upper shelves.

He caught my gaze. "Sorry. I just hadn't realized some of Avi's stuff would still be here. That's his jacket." He jerked his chin at the boots on the lower shelf—one pair of wellies and another pair of hiking boots. "His boots."

"Do you think all his other belongings are here, too?" I asked, whispering for some reason, as if we were sneaking in and didn't want to be discovered.

"Could be. He and Oren owned the house jointly, and Oren didn't return after Avi's death, so it's probably something of a time capsule.

Oh god. Rats. There are bound to be rats.

I sighed and flicked the switch next to the door. The pendulum light in the center of the mudroom flicked on. Taryn had promised to make sure the utilities were connected, and she was clearly a person who followed through on her commitments.

I took a deep breath. Dread had somehow joined the excited anticipation that had been swirling in my middle since Taryn's first call, maybe because I'd expected the house to be swept clean of its former inhabitants. Clearly it wasn't, and I decided I didn't want to face the rest of the place with only Gil for company.

"Did you spend much time here?" I asked Ricky.

He nodded. "Enough. I used to do odd jobs for Avi and Oren, especially when they were renovating the place."

I perked up a little at that. "They renovated it?"

"Yes."

Except, oh no. What if they'd stripped all the Queen Anne charm from the inside? The outside was pristine and period-appropriate, but weirder things had happened when "open plan" became the clichéd watchword for home remodeling.

Ricky must have caught my expression. "Don't worry. Oren was an architect. They did it right."

"Could you… That is, would you mind giving me the tour, then?" Despite my original desire to experience the house in a "first look" mode, with every room a surprise, now I wanted to see it with somebody who had an affection for it—or at least an affection for the men who'd lived here.

"I'd be honored." He glanced over his shoulder. "Should we bring Gilgamesh inside?"

"Probably not until I figure out where to put his litter box." I peered into his carrier. It was safely in the shade, and Gil was watching a towhee hop across the grass as though he could lure it in with his feline laser gaze alone. "He won't thank me for taking him away from bird TV right now, anyway."

"Okay, then." He pointed to the staircase. "Back stairs to the second floor and down to the basement." He jerked a thumb at the closed door on the right. "Two-car garage." Tilted his head at the gaping door on the left. "One of two powder rooms on this floor. Full baths are all upstairs."

I blinked. "Er… How many bathrooms are there?"

Ricky grinned. "Four full baths, plus the two halves."

"Six toilets?" I croaked. "That seems… excessive. Are you sure?"

He chuckled. "Trust me. I know. I had to carry one up to the attic. Come on."

He pushed open the swinging door and gestured for me to precede him.

I stepped through into a long room that had the same footprint as the mudroom. And gawked. "Holy crap."

Ricky chuckled. "I know, right? This is the butler's pantry. They redid the cabinets, so it's actually more pantry storage than prep area like an actual butler's pantry would be. Upgraded the plumbing. And you can probably tell they were big fans of natural wood."

"I can see that," I croaked as I gazed at the gorgeous cherrywood cabinetry that extended from floor to nine-foot ceiling, except on the wall with the sink and the one with a butcher block counter. "Good grief. You'd need a ladder to reach the top shelves."

He opened a tall cabinet next to the door to reveal a step ladder. "When necessary. But the plan was only to put stuff up there that didn't need constant access. There's another pantry off the kitchen, but they planned to use this one more, since it's convenient to the garage and unloading groceries."

"Right. Got it."

We stepped through a gracefully curved archway into a sunny kitchen with the same kind of cherrywood cabinetry, a long island topped with end-grain butcher block, and gleaming stainless steel appliances. Beyond the island was a circular breakfast nook nestled in one of the turrets, complete with a round table and six ladder-back chairs.

"Um, Ricky?" I pivoted slowly, probably with my mouth hanging open. "You said the place was shut up after Avi died, right?"

"Yeah," he said, his eyebrows drawing together in confusion.

"So why is everything so… so *clean*?" I swiped my finger across the granite countertop. "There's not even any dust."

He bit his lip, and even though I was sort of freaking out for a number of reasons, I could appreciate the way his white teeth dented the full flesh.

"I… don't know. I expected everything to be shrouded in dust covers, you know?" He brightened. "Taryn knew you were coming, though, right? She probably hired a cleaning service to come in and get things ready for you."

"I guess that would make sense," I said slowly. "But how did they get in? Mason bees in the locks, remember?"

He frowned for a moment, then his expression cleared. He strode back through the butler's pantry, propping the swinging door open, and flung open the garage door. He peered inside for a moment and then shot me a grin and poked something out of sight on the wall with a flourish. The garage door lifted with a hum.

"She must have the door opener, or given them the code."

I heaved a relieved sigh. It would have been nice if she'd given the code or the opener to me, although, to be fair, she didn't know exactly when I'd be arriving, and she might have tried calling after my phone died. Plus, she couldn't have known mason bees would have staged Occupy: Keyholes in both doors.

Ricky studied me, his head tilted to one side. "Does that make you feel unsafe? I know how to change the code. I can show you if you want."

I shook my head. "Maybe later. I'm fine. I'd love to see the rest of the house, and I don't want to take up too much of your time."

"No worries about that. My hours are flexible."

"What kind of hours?" I winced. "Sorry. I don't mean to be nosy, but the way your aunt, er, godmother…"

He took pity on my flailing. "She's my aunt through marriage. She married my Uncle Ramon a few years after her first husband died, but she'd been a friend of the family for years. Hence the godson relationship."

"That's why you call her Tia Sofia?"

He grinned. "Everybody in town calls her Tia Sofia. She's that kind of person. Come on. Let's see the rest of the place."

I noticed that he'd evaded my question about how he spent his time, but I let it slide for the moment because I really did want to see the rest of the house.

He led me through a family room with mission-style furniture grouped around a marble-faced fireplace and into a vaulted entry. Wide oak stairs ascended to the second-floor balcony to the left of the front door, and through a pair of french doors to the right—

"Holy *crap*!" I murmured. "An actual freaking *library*?"

There was no other word for it, because the walls were lined with floor to ceiling shelves except in the corner where a built-in desk followed half the curve of the front turret, a padded window seat upholstered in a forest green William Morris print extending the rest of the way.

I barely restrained a happy dance. Not only a library, but a *window seat*? All my latent *Jane Eyre* fantasies were coming true.

The turret windows looked out over the front lawn, the road, and the maple tree. A jewel-toned rug—ruby, dark emerald, sapphire, topaz—covered most of the oak floor, and a little wood stove was tucked next to another arch leading to what looked like a formal dining room, although it was empty of furniture.

But the bookshelves? Not empty. Not empty at all.

I ran my finger across the spines of shelf full of hardcover mysteries and thrillers. Dorothy L. Sayers. L.A. Witt and Cari Z. Conan Doyle. Jake Fields. Charlotte MacLeod.

"They left their books," I whispered.

"I think they left everything." Ricky glanced at the shelf in a way I could only describe as furtive. "Come on. There's lots more to see."

He wasn't wrong. Three bathrooms and four bedrooms on the second floor—and was I thrilled that the main suite included a sitting area in a turret? Why, yes. Yes, I was. But by the time we got to the attic, a quirky space defined by the gabled roofline, I was past thrilled and deep into gobsmacked territory.

"I can't believe this is mine." The house. The furniture. The *books*. "All my worldly possessions that didn't travel the couch-surfing circuit with me for the last two months are stored in six boxes in my ex's closet." Assuming Greg hadn't tossed them. "And now"—I flung my arms out—"*this*."

"It's a lot." Ricky stuck his hands in the pockets of his jeans and shrugged. "But good, right?"

"*So* good." I wandered over to the attic window that looked out over the back yard. A small secretary table—and yeah, I know about furniture styles because I ghostwrote for an antique dealer once—held a vintage Smith Corona electric typewriter, circa the early 70s, I'd guess, in the days before word processors or even the IBM Selectric and correcting mechanisms. "Whoever used this had to be pretty confident of their words."

"That was Avi," Ricky said softly. "He was a writer."

"Really? So am I." I grimaced. "Well, sort of."

"How can you sort of be a writer?"

"I'm a contract writer. What you'd call a ghostwriter. I vet other peoples' stories, but it's their words. Mostly."

Ricky laughed, the joyous sound somehow swallowed by the attic, even though it was mostly empty. "If you're a ghostwriter, my friend, then you've come to the right place. What better place to do ghostwriting than in Ghost?"

Chapter Five

After Ricky left, I introduced Gil to the location of his food dishes (kitchen turret) and litter box (mud room), and left him to poke around the house while I sluiced myself off in the *very* roomy tiled shower in the primary bedroom's ensuite bathroom. Afterward, I was too exhausted—both physically and emotionally—to do anything but sleep.

Despite the truly pristine state of the house—I made a mental note to thank Taryn for the cleaning service because, hey, *no rats*, much to Gil's disapprobation—I didn't feel right yet sleeping in the king-sized oak sleigh bed that had belonged to two men who'd never had a real chance to enjoy their home.

Instead, I inflated the air mattress that had been my constant companion for the last couple of months and slept in my sleeping bag in the suite's turret sitting room. I'd fallen asleep gazing at the stars, with Gil curled, purring, at my side.

I was woken by a sharp pain in my hipbone. "Ow."

I blinked blearily, disoriented for a moment, not remembering where I was. Windows just lightening with dawn surrounded me, and maple leaves fluttered against the panes with a gentle *shush*ing.

My house. I was in *my house.*

But overnight, my air mattress had finally given up the ghost—*heh*—and deflated. My bony hips didn't approve of the oak floor, nor, when I crawled out of my sleeping bag and stood up, did my back or my knees. Clearly I'd have to get over my squeamishness about the bed. Or should I say beds, because every bedroom on the second floor had one. I just needed to *pick* one and sleep in it tonight.

After I brushed my teeth and washed my face—I'd save showering until after at least one cup of coffee—I pulled a couple of sets of sheets from the neat stacks in the linen closet. After all, I wasn't going to refuse to use them. I was broke, not boneheaded, and these had a higher thread count than I'd ever seen in my life. Besides, thrift stores had been my main shopping venues even before the Greg debacle. I was used to *used*.

Blessing Uncle Oren for locating the laundry facilities on the second floor rather than downstairs or in the basement, and Avi for keeping the detergent well-stocked, I tossed the sheets in the washer. Yeah, they seemed clean and smelled fine, but they'd been sitting in that closet for ten years.

And they'd belonged to somebody else.

So washing them was a sort of ritual of new ownership, I guess.

I headed down the stairs, Gil scampering in front of me rather than winding himself around my ankles in his usual morning attempt to murder me for not feeding him early enough. But when I got to the last step, he was standing in the middle of the vestibule in a double arch—back and tail—looking at least twice as big as normal with all his fur standing out.

I hurried over to him. "What's—"

My jaw dropped, because beyond him, the library looked as though it had been hit by a tornado. Most of the shelves were empty now because books littered the floor, completely obscuring the rug.

My heart caught in my throat because in addition to the books—whether spine up, opened face down, or closed—the place was papered with, well, *paper*. I picked up one sheet, my hand shaking. Page 287/288 from Jake Fields' latest thriller. I spotted the cover—hardcover edition—upside down in the corner, only a couple of pages still remaining. In a way, I could commiserate—the book hadn't lived up to the earlier books by a long shot—but that wasn't the point.

Someone had been in my house.

While I was asleep upstairs.

They'd been in here and they'd destroyed things, things that, while I was still getting used to them belonging to *me,* definitely didn't belong to some vandal.

How the hell had they gotten in? I froze. Could they still be here? And had they done any other damage? I hadn't heard anything overnight, but I sleep pretty soundly once I finally drop off.

I backed out of the library and crept into the family room. The throw pillows were scattered over the area rug and one of the paintings—a landscape featuring Mount Hood—hung crooked on the wall, but nothing had been broken that I could see. I wouldn't be able to tell if anything was missing. I'd barely looked at the place, let alone taken an inventory.

I grabbed the poker from the fireplace set and scuttled back to the front door. The deadbolt was thrown, just as I'd left it last night. I flipped its brass thumb-turn and stepped onto the porch. Realizing I was still clutching page 287/288, I folded it about six times and wedged it between the door and the frame so I didn't do anything stupid like lock myself out.

The many double-hung windows that opened onto the porch all *seemed* secure and undamaged, so I went inside again and checked the back door and all the other first-floor windows.

All locked tight.

I peeked in the garage where my Civic sat in dusty solitude. It appeared undisturbed, although if somebody had gotten in with the opener or the code, I wouldn't be able to tell.

I eyed the basement stairs. The basement was one place Ricky hadn't taken me yesterday. He'd offered, but I'd declined because by that time I was in total sensory overload and who knew what was down there?

I glanced at Gil, who was plastered against my leg, nose twitching as though testing the air with his olfactory rodent radar. His fur had mostly flattened by now, although his tail was still in bottlebrush mode.

"We've got to check, Gil. If you see a rat"—*ugh, no*—"you are *not* to engage. You don't know where they've been."

I scooped him up in one arm, gripping the poker with the other, and crept downstairs.

I'm not sure what I expected, but it wasn't this. The basement, while not what any real estate agent would call *finished,* wasn't a serial killer's murder dungeon or dank hoarder's den. It was well lit from one concrete wall to the other, nothing obscuring the sight lines except supporting posts.

The neatest, most immaculate workshop I'd ever seen was laid out along two of its walls, power tools like a table saw and a drill press bolted to the concrete floor. Empty metal shelving lined the other two walls. In other words, zero places for anyone to hide.

When I checked the bulkhead doors, they were still bolted from the inside, just as Carson had said they'd be.

I set Gil on his feet and he sniffed around the room in a desultory way, but not with the focus he reserved for hunting furred or feathered victims, and not with anything like his response when we first came downstairs. From my own observations and his reaction, I assumed there was nothing to see down here unless I wanted to take up woodworking sometime in the future. I patted my leg and Gil trotted over. I picked him up and went upstairs, turning off the basement lights and shutting the door behind me.

The kitchen hadn't been touched. I hesitated to go upstairs. I mean, was there a point? It was the second story, and I'd been there, albeit sacked out in one turreted corner. But I'd ghostwritten a retired detective's memoir, and I'd learned never to assume: If somebody wanted to get into a house badly enough, they'd get in. There were such things as ladders, after all.

So I went back upstairs and checked every freaking window, including the ones in the turret that had surrounded me all night. I'd opened a couple of them to enjoy the breeze, but their screens hadn't been touched, at least not as far as I could tell. Nothing in any of the bedrooms had been disturbed, nor was anybody hiding in the closets.

I paused at the stairs leading to the attic.

If somebody was lurking up there, they could take me out before I knew what—literally—hit me. But they could have done the same thing while I was asleep, too. I took a deep breath, along with a tighter grip on my trusty poker, and stomped upstairs.

"I'm coming up now," I called. "If anyone's there, I just want to talk. Assuming you don't want to kill me. Because if that's the case, I'm not hanging around for the convo."

Nothing. No sound except the cheep of birdsong filtering in from the open windows in the main suite. Gil scampered up ahead of me, tail up, apparently perfectly content to check out the accommodations. I stopped when my head topped the floor and peered around. The attic was dimmer than downstairs because the only windows were in the dormers and they were smaller than the ones on the first two floors. I didn't *see* anything moving, and Gil was *mrrp*ing happily, pawing at a stray sunbeam that shone through the window that overlooked the backyard.

I sighed and trudged up the last few steps to check inside the only door—full bathroom, containing nothing but gleaming tile and porcelain—before joining Gil. He'd parked his furry butt in his sunbeam and was staring fixedly at the secretary.

"Not that I doubt your feline superpowers, Gil, but not even you could bat that typewriter off the table. Those things were made to…"

Spiders—the phantom kind—staged a kick line up my spine.

Yesterday, the Smith-Corona's platen had been empty, but now? A piece of onionskin paper was rolled onto it, as though awaiting a missing typist. I crept forward. The machine held no ribbon, but since the keys on this model struck with some force, that didn't mean the totally blank paper held no message.

With other tips from my retired detective client skittering around in my brain, I covered my hand with my T-shirt and rolled the page free. Then I high-tailed it downstairs again, Gil bounding at my heels.

"Pencil, pencil, pencil," I muttered as I yanked open drawers in the kitchen. "Oh, come on. Who doesn't keep a pencil or two in their kitchen?"

There was probably one in the library desk, but I didn't want to go back in there until the police had been here—and, yes, I was definitely calling the police, even though my client had told me that cold burglaries had a very low clearance rate. In hindsight, I should probably have called them before I went slinking around the house with a freaking fireplace poker like some TSTL teenager in a slasher movie.

"Aha!" In the corner drawer by a telephone niche, I found one of those big, rectangular carpenter's pencils, apparently sharpened with a knife. I set the paper on the counter and, holding it down with one hand, carefully ran the pencil over its surface.

The phantom spiders staged an encore, because sure enough, the impression of the keys was there, embedded in the paper:

no no no no no no no no no

Chapter Six

Leaving Gil with his morning kibble, I grabbed my recharged phone and sprinted out the front door and down the porch steps. Someone had been in *my house*. Someone had been in my house long enough to trash my library and leave threatening messages on a typewriter with no ribbon.

I wasn't happy about my list of possible suspects. For one thing, it included an unknowable number of cleaners. For another, it included the cute guy who'd appealed to me more than anyone in years—including Greg—as well as the only living relative of the previous owner, and the probate attorney. I mean, seriously? Could the universe have thumbed its nose at me any more clearly?

Here, Maz, have a house. Oh, by the way, somebody clearly doesn't want you in it.

I glanced up and down the street, although what I expected to see, I couldn't say. It's not like the burglar would have hung around, waiting for me to threaten him with my poker. Which I had left inside, anyway. I caught a movement out of the corner of my eye. That same pale, bespectacled face, like a studious owl, peered out at me from the window of the Craftsman house next door. When they saw me looking, they twitched the curtains across the window.

Okay, maybe there was another suspect: Creepy neighbor who wasn't keen on having an ethnic kid next door. I refused to suspect Tia Sofia. For one thing, she wouldn't have been able to reach the top library shelves. For another, Gil liked her.

Although that may be more related to her giving him a metric ton of kitty treats.

I sighed. First thing, call Ricky and somehow nonchalantly inquire whether he'd come back during his *flexible* hours and vandalized my house. Yeah, not exactly a meet-cute, by any stretch of the imagination. I had Carson's number on his business card. As Avi's cousin, somebody who'd grown up around this house, he'd be the most likely candidate to know who else might have a key to the place. And no matter what he'd said, I didn't believe any kid worth his Playstation wouldn't know the best secret ways in and out of a house. Then there were Taryn and the mysterious cleaners.

But as I was scrolling through my contacts to find Ricky's number, a silver Prius drew up to the curb in front of me and a woman in a burgundy pantsuit climbed out of the car. She was maybe six inches shorter than me, but her elaborate crown of braided locs made her a little taller. Her warm brown skin practically glowed with health, and when she smiled at me, dimples popped in her round cheeks. "Hi. You must be Maz. I'm Taryn."

I tucked my phone away and raised one hand in a half-hearted excuse for a wave. "Yeah, that's me."

She strode around the front of her car and I was interested to note that she wore black Doc Martens with her raw silk suit. "I'm sorry I wasn't here to welcome you. I tried to call and get an ETA, but it went to voicemail."

"Yeah, my phone died about an hour and a half out of town."

"Ricky let me know you'd arrived, though, and that he'd given you the tour." She grinned, and despite myself, I smiled back. "Well? What do you think?"

"To tell you the truth, I'm not sure *what* to think."

Her wide brow pleated. "What do you mean?"

I held up both hands. "Don't get me wrong. The house is amazing, and I'm still pinching myself that it somehow belongs to me. But…" I huffed out a breath. "Come in?"

She nodded, although she didn't completely lose the frown. When we stepped inside, Gil immediately galloped over and stood at her feet, looking up at her. "Oh, my. Look at you." She crouched down, seemingly unconcerned about the amount of ginger fur wafting onto her burgundy pants. "Aren't you the handsome boy?" She glanced up at me. "His name?"

"Gilgamesh. Gil. And I'm not sure when he became such a flirt. Usually he disdains all strangers, but he was downright polite to Ricky and actually *purred* for Tia Sofia. He hated my ex-boyfriend."

She flashed me a grin as she gave Gil one last skritch and stood up, brushing her hands on her slacks and decorating them with more ginger fur. "What can I tell you? He's obviously a good judge of character."

I thought about Greg and his latest passive-aggressive shenanigans. "Yeah. I probably should have listened to him the first time he hissed at the jerk."

She tilted her head. "I'm guessing you didn't invite me in here just to meet your cat."

"That would be a no." I gestured to the library doors. "Take a look at what greeted me this morning."

She stepped past me, expertly evading Gil's attempt to trip her by flopping in front of her feet, and looked inside. Her eyes widened, and she shot a look at me that I couldn't interpret. "You found it like this?"

Was that accusation in her tone? Did she think *I'd* do something like this to a house that I'd lived in for less than twenty-four hours? "Yes. I came downstairs around 6:30 or so. I never heard anything. I slept in the main suite, although on the floor in the turret."

She hunkered down again, prompting Gil to try to climb onto her knee. She petted him absently as she gingerly lifted one of the torn pages. She studied it. "Is this the only book that was destroyed?"

I nodded. "Others might have been damaged a little from being tossed around, but that's the only one that had its pages ripped out, as far as I can tell."

"Interesting." She shifted Gil aside and stood. "Is this all?"

I glared at her. "Isn't it enough? I mean, *look* at it."

She raised both palms in a placating gesture. "I'm not belittling it, trust me. I'm just trying to determine the full scope. Did you call the police?"

"Not yet. I was about to, but..." I bit my lip and glanced away.

"What is it?"

I sighed. "The thing is, I just got into town. I'm barely moved in. I don't know anything about what the environment is here. I mean, aren't most small towns pretty insular? Don't they close ranks against strangers and newcomers?"

The corners of her lips twitched. "Ghost has its idiosyncrasies, but corrupt, bigoted law enforcement isn't one of them. We don't have a town police force, just one of the county deputies who's stationed here, but she's a good sort, and the sheriff believes in the rule of law."

"Good to know. But what I mean is, if I were to... cast aspersions on anybody when they're well known in town and I'm a cypher? Let's just say I'm planning to make this my home. I don't want to get off on the wrong foot by making enemies my first day."

"What aspersions would those be?"

"Well..." I swallowed convulsively. "The only people who know I'm here are you, Ricky, Sofia, and the person next door who keeps peeking through her curtains at me. Oh, and Carson." I grimaced. "Actually, his welcome is what made me dial into the we-don't-want-your-kind-here cliche."

Her brows drew together. "Why? What did he do?"

I laughed weakly. "He mistook me for a burglar when I was trying to get in the front door and threatened to tase me."

She rolled her eyes. "I'm not sure Carson owns a Taser. But I'm sorry that was your introduction to Ghost. We're actually a pretty friendly place. Sofia and Ricky are much more the norm than Carson, especially since he moved to Richdale to open his real estate practice."

"What about"—I jerked my thumb at the Craftsman—"the window peeper?"

This time, she laughed, a full, rolling belly laugh that would have fit somebody twice her size. "That's Professor DeHaven. Patrice."

My eyebrows shot up. "Professor? Professor of what? Covert surveillance?"

"No. She's actually an adjunct professor of parapsychology at Richdale University."

"Parapsychology? You mean, like ESP and voices from beyond the grave?"

She waggled one hand. "Among other things."

"Is that even a thing?"

"It is in Ghost and Richdale. Patrice also owns the needlework-slash-occult shop in town."

I narrowed my eyes. "Needlework and occult are not exactly two words I expect to find sharing shop space."

Taryn sighed. "They didn't used to. They used to be two separate shops, but Ghost businesses have been struggling a little since the bypass out of Richdale opened a few years ago. We don't get as many beach-goers stopping on the way to the coast anymore. Patrice's mother owned the needlework place and her aunt owned the occult shop. But after Mrs. DeHaven passed, the aunt moved to Portland. Patrice didn't want to deprive Ghost of two businesses at once, so she combined them and hired a manager to run them for her."

"Someone adept at psychic knitting?" I asked dryly.

She grinned. "You'd be surprised. But while Patrice kept the businesses open, she's a dyed-in-the-wool introvert. When she's at home, she keeps to herself to recharge for teaching her classes."

I suppose I could sympathize. My grandmother had been an introvert too, and spent much of her last couple of years happily never leaving her apartment. "Well, it's a little freaky, her peering out the window. All I can see is those round glasses glinting behind the window, like—"

"Mrs. Who," we both said simultaneously and grins broke out on both our faces.

"You read *A Wrinkle in Time*?" she asked.

"From the time I was in grade school. I was so excited when they announced the movie, and the casting for Meg was perfect. But—"

"But not the three ladies." She wrinkled her nose. "Ugh. I wonder if the name actresses refused to play the parts if they couldn't glam it up." She shook her head. "Tangents aside, was there anything else?"

"Some throw pillows were tossed around in the family room, and a painting is askew. But otherwise, the only thing"—there went those spiders again, my own personal arachnid Rockettes —"was on the typewriter in the attic."

She frowned. "Typewriter in the attic? The only time I was in the attic, it was packed to the rafters with dusty cardboard boxes and chairs with their cane bottoms broken. Granted, that was when I was thirteen."

"They must have cleared it out when they did the renovation. Now, it's cleaner than my old apartment, and the only thing that's in there is a Smith Corona electric with no ribbon on top of a Mission-style secretary."

Something flickered in her eyes. "Show me."

"The typewriter? Or the paper that was on it?"

"Did you remove the paper?"

"Yeah. I brought it downstairs."

"I wish you hadn't done that," she murmured, then sighed. "Okay. Show me the paper."

I led her into the kitchen and pointed to the paper on the counter. "There. The typewriter didn't have a ribbon, but the keys still made an impression."

She didn't touch the page, just stared down at the freaky message:

no no no no no no no no no

When she looked up at me, her dark eyes shone with excitement. "Maz, I don't think you had a burglar."

"Are you kidding? Then how do you explain the mess in the library?"

She rolled her lips together, clearly weighing her response. "Could you discover how they got inside?"

I huffed. "The only thing I can figure is that they came in through the garage. Which reminds me—thanks for arranging the cleaning service, but could you return the garage opener to me?"

Her forehead puckered. "Cleaning service?"

"Yeah. The place was spotless—and I mean *spotless*. Even the refrigerator and oven sparkled like new. So whoever you hired did a great job—unless one of their employees got it into their head to stage a little mayhem."

She took a deep breath. "Maz. I think you should sit down."

For some reason, her gentle tone freaked me out nearly as much as Patrice peering through her curtains. I scooped up Gil and cradled him against my chest for comfort. "Why?"

"Please? Sit?"

I huffed again, but stalked over to sit at the breakfast table, settling Gil on my knee. "Okay. I'm sitting."

She sat down across from me, folding her hands on the table. "I didn't arrange a cleaning service."

I just stared at her. "But the house was clean. Could someone else have arranged it? Carson? He did show up when I arrived. Maybe he has a key, or the code to the garage." Although if he had, why hadn't he told me so when he'd met me on the porch?

"Since Avi was his cousin, maybe he's been taking care of the place."

She shook her head. "Yes, they were cousins, but they weren't close. Carson resented Avi for… well, never mind why, but Avi would never have entrusted a key to Carson."

"Ricky, then," I said, a little wildly, because I did *not* like where this conversation was going. "He keeps the outside pristine. And he knows his way around a lock. He could have gotten inside…"

Except Ricky had been just as surprised at the state of the house as I'd been. Unless he was a really good actor. Plus, he said he knew how to change the garage door code.

But Taryn shook her head again. "He wouldn't come inside, not without an invitation."

"Then who? Damn it, Taryn, somebody came into my house while I was asleep and vandalized it. They could have vandalized me too, because I never heard them. *Somebody* did it, because I certainly didn't."

She nodded slowly. "Maz, have you wondered why this town is called Ghost?"

I reared back in my chair, causing Gil to dig his claws through my jeans and into my leg. "No. No no no no no." Jeez, I sounded like the mysterious typewriter message. "I am *not* living in a haunted house. I was *not* vandalized by a freaking *ghost*!"

"Then how else can you explain it?"

"I don't know." My eyes were probably bugging out of my head by this time. "A conspiracy? Maybe everyone in town is in on it, trying to drive me away so the other heirs can take possession. I mean, the will was contested, right?"

"Both of them. There are still issues that have to be resolved, which we can go over at my office as soon as you've got your feet under you here, but those aren't related to anyone who lives in Ghost."

"I don't care. This is reality. Reality is… concrete. It's finite. It has *rules*. And those rules don't include freaking *ghosts* popping out of the freaking *beyond* to trash my freaking *house*!"

She reached across the table and laid her hand over mine, which was clutching the edge of the table as though I were Kate Winslet and it was the only thing keeping me from going down with the *Titanic*.

"Maz, it's not that bad."

"No?" I jerked my hand out from under hers and jabbed a finger toward her. "Then you're saying this whole thing is an elaborate prank? Because I've gotta tell you, I've always *despised* April Fool's Day, and besides, that was two weeks ago."

"It's not a prank or a practical joke." Her smile was almost incandescent. "What it is, I think, is the thing that will save the town and put Ghost back on the map."

I crumpled, dropping my forehead against the table. *"No no no no no no no no no."* Yeah, the typewriter knew what it was talking about.

"If it's okay with you, I'd like to invite a couple of people over to meet you and see this."

I rolled my head enough that I could glare at her out of one eye. "See what? Me having a nervous breakdown?"

"No. The library. The typewritten message. The house." She ducked so she could meet my gaze. "I think it will help. I promise."

What other option did I have? Move back to Portland for another round of couch surfing? Gil had hated that. Pretend like nothing was happening, and wait for the other shoe to drop and the destruction to escalate? I'd seen *Amityville Horror*. I knew *that* wouldn't end well.

But if I was thinking about horror movies, I'd probably crossed the threshold into provisional paranormal believer. Might as well lean into it.

"Who you gonna call?"

"One of my dads. Saul Pasternak. He's the executive director of Richdale Manor, Ghost's answer to the Winchester Mystery House." She smiled wryly. "And Patrice DeHaven. It's time to pull in the experts."

Chapter Seven

Saul Pasternak was a tanned, rangy man with a shock of snowy hair, a beak of a nose, and the gentlest smile I'd ever seen. He looked just like Sam Waterston in *Grace & Frankie*, and since I'd always loved that actor, he set me at ease immediately.

Patrice DeHaven, on the other hand? Pale as a...well, ghost, with a wrist-thick salt-and-pepper braid hanging between her prominent shoulder blades? I'm not sure she *could* smile. Not that she seemed angry or menacing or disapproving. Focused, that was the professor. Intense. But while she didn't precisely *relax* me like Saul did, I never got the feeling she was trying to snow me, either. She didn't have an ounce of New Age woo-woo about her. Actually, she reminded me a little of Egon Spengler, Harold Ramis's character from *Ghostbusters*. Serious about the work, you know?

Even if the work was something I still had major doubts about.

I sat on the front stairs, Gil on my lap, while Saul and Patrice surveyed the library. They'd photographed the whole place thoroughly first, then started picking through the book carnage, speaking to one another in low voices. Saul jotted things on a tablet as Patrice picked up each book and set it back on a shelf based on some criteria she didn't share with me. She was also gathering the scattered pages of *Borderline*, the destroyed Fields book, slotting them into page number order and stacking them neatly on the desk.

Taryn emerged from the kitchen and handed me a steaming cup. I sniffed at the steam. "What's this?"

"Chamomile tea." She settled next to me with her own cup and Gil immediately slunk onto to her lap, the traitor. "I figured you could do with something calming."

"What I could do with is a stiff drink. Or maybe ten." But I took a sip of the tea. The warmth was comforting, anyway, combating the chill that had descended on me once I realized these people actually believed a ghost had vandalized my house.

"There's a pub in town. I'll take you down there in a bit and stand you at least a couple of rounds." She nudged my shoulder. "Although we should probably wait until at least lunchtime for that."

I glanced at her sidelong. "Do you really believe this could be ghost-related?"

She gazed down into her cup, her fingers cradling its bowl and laced through its handle. "You have to understand, Maz. I grew up here. My dads both grew up here. We were raised on the tales of Thaddeus Richdale and his quest to reach beyond the veil."

"Richdale? Like the town?"

She nodded. "His father, Josiah, was a blacksmith who parlayed his smithy into a fortune supplying 49ers with shovels and pans during the gold rush, which convinced his son that only fools chased anything as chancy as gold."

"Wait. Gold was chancy, but ghosts were a safe bet?"

"Ghosts were Thaddeus's thing. Josiah's thing was money. Money and paranoia. He moved his family up here after the gold rush ended, convinced that everyone in Sacramento was trying to rob him."

"And people in Oregon weren't?"

Taryn smirked. "They'd have had to find him—and his money—first. When he parked his family here, there weren't any people around for miles. The isolation probably sent all of them a little loony. After Josiah passed suddenly, Thaddeus became convinced that he'd hidden half his fortune somewhere. He became obsessed with finding a way to reach beyond the grave and shake the truth out of him."

"I take it he didn't succeed?"

"Not for lack of trying. He built Richdale Manor as a mirror of the Winchester Mystery House because he'd heard Sarah Winchester had succeeded in contacting spirits. He started Richdale University—although it was only Richdale College then—and endowed it with the proviso that half the income would go to the parapsychology and paranormal studies departments, and should either of those departments be shut down, his money would immediately be withdrawn from the school and held in trust for the person who finally discovered Josiah's hidden treasure."

"I take it nobody's managed that either."

"Frankly? I don't think there ever was a hidden treasure."

"Ah," I said, tapping the side of my nose. "Daddy issues."

She snorted a laugh. "Something like that."

"So why is the college in Richdale, but Richdale Manor is here in Ghost?" It was, in fact, across the street from my house—what I'd taken for a park.

She shrugged. "Josiah wanted an estate. A big one."

"So nobody could get close enough to steal his money?"

"Yep. But he needed a population center to supply his family's needs, so Richdale grew beyond his property line. Our town built up around the manor later, as Thaddeus sold off parcels of land in his never-ending attempt to keep up with Sarah Winchester."

"Did he name the town Ghost?"

She smiled crookedly. "No. That was something the first townspeople started."

"Because the place was haunted?"

"No. Actually, because Thaddeus Richdale turned into a virtual ghost himself, getting more and more desperate to crack the secret of the beyond before he passed through the veil himself."

"So—" I gestured to Saul and Patrice, who'd cleared enough of the mess that the library rug's jewel tones peeked out between the books and papers that still remained. "—care to explain their attitude?"

"Thaddeus never succeeded, but he left the Manor in trust to the town, provided they continue to search for proof of the hereafter."

"And the treasure, presumably."

"Pfft." She waved a hand. "Nobody takes that seriously anymore. The Manor's a museum now—Dad is the director—but finding proof has turned into something of a town hobby. We're proud of it, of our relationship to the University and its paranormal studies program. We're proud of being the town that never stops looking. But we've never found evidence." She nodded toward the library. "Until now."

"I'm still not convinced," I grumbled.

She cocked an eyebrow. "You'd rather believe you slept through *living* people slinging books around the house and tromping up and down stairs while you snored through the whole thing?"

I shivered. "Don't. I hate that idea, but I'm not sure having a ghost perp is any better. Maybe worse." I sighed. "I shouldn't complain, because"—I spread my hands, my tea sloshing a little in the cup—"I've got a freaking *house*." I slanted a glance at her. "I don't suppose Uncle Oren left me any actual cash for its upkeep? Or my upkeep, for that matter?"

She grimaced. "That's one of the things that's still in contention, although it dates back to Avi's estate rather than Oren's specifically. Avi was a writer."

I nodded. "Ricky told me."

"There's a lawsuit outstanding involving one of his books, and until it's settled, his royalties are frozen."

"Any idea how soon that could happen?"

She waggled her hand until Gil batted at it to get her to return to her most important duty—petting him. "Hard to tell. It's complicated."

"In that case, I need to find some work."

"What do you do?"

I squinted at her. "Don't laugh."

"You know the best way to get somebody to laugh? Tell them not to."

"Fine." I huffed out a breath. "I'm a ghostwriter."

She wanted to laugh. I could tell by the way her eyes crinkled when she pressed her lips together. But she managed to control herself. "Any particular genre?"

I shrugged. "Nothing too technical. I'm not your guy if you're writing a treatise on nuclear physics. But fiction, memoir, self-help, anything that relies on narrative clarity and basic research rather than in-depth scientific knowledge. I can match anyone's voice. Or give them one if they can't locate their own with a microscope."

"Hmmm." She set her cup on the stairs and pulled her phone out of her blazer pocket, despite Gil being draped across her legs like a hairy ginger throw rug. She swiped an app and thumbed something faster than I could touch-type on my laptop. "There."

"There what?"

"I posted your profile on Ghostline."

"Ghostline?"

"Town chat room. If anyone has a job, or knows someone who has a job, or knows someone who *knows* someone who has a job, they'll get in touch." She bumped her shoulder with mine. "We might be a small town, but we can network like nobody's business, and the internet is everywhere."

"Thanks, but I might not be able to wait for the word to spread. If I don't get something soon, I'll—"

Her phone beeped. She smirked at me and held it up. "Three responses already. That soon enough for you?"

I had to laugh. "Thanks. It's still not a done deal, though. I'll need to talk to them about the projects, see if I'm right for them. I've got one possibility in the pipeline, but I really don't want to accept it."

"Why not?"

"Because it's a terrible book. This guy is convinced that his memoir will be a best seller, but he's one of the most boring people I've ever met. Not even I can make his life sound interesting. And when the book tanks—and it will—I'll get the blame and my professional rep will take another hit."

"Then don't take it."

I pointed at her phone. "Despite your efforts, things take time and I must keep Gil in the style to which he's become accustomed. Oh, and I might need to eat too."

She screwed up her face. "Hmmm." Then she looked at the two people in the library. "Hey, Dad?"

Saul looked up. "Yes, dear?"

"Weren't you planning to write up Thaddeus's story for the museum?"

"Yes, but I haven't found the time."

She made jazz hands at me. "May I present Maz Amani, ghostwriter, who just happens to have room in his busy schedule?"

Saul smiled, making him look even more like Sam Waterston. "Really? Do you handle research as well?"

"Uh…" My gaze bounced between the two of them. "Well. Yes. I can give you my rates and a writing sample—"

He waved my words away. "I'm not concerned about that. Just collecting all Thaddeus's papers and getting them in order would be worth whatever you want to charge. And if we move forward with the book? Even better."

"Dad," Taryn said, her tone both fond and exasperated. "That's not the way to negotiate the best deal."

He winked at her. "I leave all the negotiations to you, my dear." He turned away when Patrice said something to him.

Taryn grinned. "That's settled. You've got a gig. What are your rates?" I told her and she shook her head. "Honestly, you and my dad are a pair." She shifted Gil off her lap, earning her a *mew* of displeasure. "Don't worry. I'll draw up a contract that's fair to you both." She stood up. "In fact, I'll head into the office right now to get it taken care of." She opened the front door. "But meet me later at the pub and I'll stand you that drink."

"Taryn," somebody said from outside, "I don't know how you can do me like that."

Chapter Eight

That voice…

I scrambled to my feet. Sure enough, Ricky was standing on the porch, apparently about to knock. I couldn't help the little thrill in my middle, despite him remaining on my short list of break-in suspects. Because the whole ghost thing? Still not buying it, but I couldn't deny Ricky was dang cute.

Although in case you haven't noticed? My taste in men could use some work.

"Um. Hi." I flapped my second pathetic wave of the day, then wiped my hands on my jeans.

He smiled warmly at me and that thrill amped up. "Good morning. I was just dropping off Tia's groceries and thought I'd see how your first night in the new place went. Then I find one of my oldest friends steering you toward a rival business instead of Taqueria Vargas, home of the best Mexican food in Ghost and run, incidentally, by my family."

Taryn rolled her eyes. "He needed a drink, Enrique. Not dinner."

Ricky clapped a hand to his chest. "And Papi's margaritas don't fill the bill?"

"Let's let Maz decide, okay? Maybe he doesn't like Mexican food." She glanced at me. "Although the Taqueria's food is amazing. His papi knows his way around a kitchen. So what'll it be? Pub grub or Mexican?"

"I love Mexican. Food. Mexican food. Yes. That." Oh, yeah. I was just exactly that smooth. I snatched Gil up before he could run out the door.

"Good. Enrique can tell you how to get there—it's on Main Street, like most everything else in town. Shall we say six?"

"Sounds good to me," I said.

"I'll have that contract for you by then, too." She leaned back to peer into the library. "Bye, Dad. I'll see you and Pop for dinner on Sunday. Bye, Professor." She skritched Gil's ears. "Goodbye, Gil." With one waggle of her fingers to me, she strode across the porch and down the steps toward her Prius.

Ricky watched her go with a shake of his head. "She's a powerhouse, that one. Has been all her life." He faced me. "And once you land in her friend zone, you've got a champion forever."

"Good to know." I beckoned for him to come in and shut the door behind him so I could set Gil on his feet.

"Did she say Saul was here? Why? Usually, he's at the museum by this time. Professor DeHaven too?"

I glanced at him a little sharply. It occurred to me that if the town of Ghost was truly jonesing for an actual haunting, maybe staging one with a naïve newbie—and one who was a writer—was a way to boost the town's mystique. Ricky seemed genuinely curious, but hey, Greg had fooled me at first, too.

"Yeah. There was an… incident." I gestured toward the library. "Take a look."

Ricky shot me a quizzical glance and strode forward. When he reached the french doors, he rocked back on his heels. "Whoa."

Saul looked up from his tablet, his lined face practically glowing. "Isn't it wonderful?"

"I'm not sure that's the word I'd use," I muttered.

Ricky edged into the room, peering around at the shelves that had been neat and full yesterday, and the papers that still littered the floor, despite the tidy stack Professor DeHaven had collected on the desk. He looked at me, and I could swear there was concern and not triumph in his dark eyes. Trust me—after three years with Greg, I could tell the difference.

"Did somebody break in? I knew I should have changed that garage code yesterday. If I—"

"No, no," Saul said around a deep chuckle. "We're almost certain it was a manifestation. Not only psychokinetic force and possible vortex, but actual direct writing with a cogent message. No ectoplasm, but we can't have everything."

Professor DeHaven gave a noncommittal grunt and added three more pages to the stack.

Ricky reached out as though to grip my arm, but dropped his hand to his side. *Damn it.* "Are you okay?"

I shrugged. "I'm not sure which is more alarming. That I slept through somebody breaking into my house or that said house might be haunted by a literary critic."

Ricky turned to Saul. "What was the message?"

Saul fixed me with a gaze like a hopeful grade-schooler asking his parents for money for the ice cream truck. "May I show him? Or would you rather do it?"

I held up my palms. "Be my guest."

Saul left Professor DeHaven collecting the deconstructed novel and bustled out of the library and through the family room, Ricky at his heels with Gil trotting behind, tail in the air. I trailed them like a cranky caboose.

"I never expected that our first manifestation would be *here*," Saul tossed over his shoulder. "I always expected it to be at the Manor. It's the place with the seance room, after all, and the building layout and construction materials are precisely configured to capture etheric energy."

I leaned against the doorway, my arms crossed. "What's etheric energy?"

Ricky's lips quirked. He flicked a finger at my Star Wars T-shirt. "Kind of like the Force."

I smiled back involuntarily. "Which side? Dark or light?"

He shrugged. "Who knows? Since nobody's ever managed to define it *or* harness it."

"Then how do you know the Manor is configured to capture it?" I asked Saul, intrigued despite myself. I mean, the Force was something I could understand, if only in a purely fictional way.

"He doesn't," Ricky said, while Saul was still searching for words. "Nobody does. But they never stop trying."

"Never mind, never mind," Saul said. "Just *look*, Ricky." He angled the typewriter paper toward Ricky with the tip of one finger.

Ricky's expression changed from indulgent to sharp in an instant, his brows snapping together. "Where did this come from?"

I pointed toward the ceiling. "It was, um, on the typewriter in the attic."

Ricky's narrow-eyed gaze was almost accusatory. "The typewriter didn't have any paper in it yesterday."

"I *know*," I snapped. "And the library didn't look like the aftermath of a cyclone either, but here we are." I ran my hands through my hair, no doubt making my curls stick out. "Now do you see why I need a drink?"

"Yeah." Ricky's expression cleared and he heaved a sigh. "I think we all do."

"Excellent!" Saul clapped his hands together. "I'll break out the champagne."

CHAPTER NINE

Ricky and Taryn were right about one thing: The food at Taqueria Vargas was outstanding. I leaned back on the wooden banquette and rubbed my stomach. "That was the most incredible cochinita pibil I've ever tasted."

"Told you," Ricky said, topping up my margarita and Taryn's from the pitcher in the middle of the table. "Best Mexican Restaurant in Ghost."

Taryn took a sip of her drink. "It's the only one in Ghost."

Ricky shrugged and brandished his glass with a grin. "That means nobody can argue with me. I mean, if you make other claims—best in the state, best north of the border, best west of the Mississippi—there'll always be somebody to argue with you." He sniffed, putting on a snooty expression. "Even if they're *obviously* wrong."

I traced the grain on the polished wood tabletop with a finger and sighed.

"Maz?" Taryn said. "You okay? Were the terms of the contract acceptable?"

I glanced up, my vision only *slightly* impaired by how many margaritas I'd consumed so far. "The contract's great. Very generous."

Taryn snorted. "You haven't seen the chaos of Thaddeus's papers. Once you do, you'll probably demand double the rate."

"Triple," Ricky said. "Minimum."

"I'm sure it can't be that bad. I'll head over there tomorrow to start sorting through everything."

"So if it's not the contract, what is it?"

I chewed on my lower lip, my gaze drifting from one of them to the other. "What if my house really *is* haunted? I mean, people have been driven out of their homes by vengeful spirits —"

"*Alleged* vengeful spirits," Ricky said.

"Okay, *alleged* vengeful spirits. But whether they were real or not—"

"They weren't," Taryn said. "Never been proven."

"*Fine.* Real or not, they still drove people out of their homes, and guys, I've got nowhere else to go."

"Oh, Maz." Taryn set her glass down with a *clink*. "You're part of the town now. One of us. You won't be homeless."

"Yeah, but I've ridden the couch surfing wave before and I really don't want to dive back into it. I want a house. I want a *home,* and I really thought I'd found one. But somebody or something doesn't want me to have it."

Taryn studied me, her head tilted to the side as she drummed her fingernails on the table. I noticed her nails were on the short side, but her manicure was perfect, with a jeweled pattern on her thumbnail. An interesting blend of practical and stylish, Taryn. "We don't know that. Nothing hurt *you*."

"Yet," I muttered, and took a gulp of my margarita. "I'm kind of afraid of what I'll find when I go back." I'd agreed with Saul and Patrice's request to install a ribbon in the Smith Corona after we'd found a stash of them in the library desk and roll in a fresh sheet of paper, but I really didn't want to wake up and hear the keys clacking overhead.

"Do you want someone to stay with you?" Ricky asked. "Either one of us would be glad to do it."

I considered that through my margarita haze. I still hadn't given up the notion of a completely human answer to the vandalism, and as much as I liked Ricky and Taryn, they were still two of the people who could have had perfectly ordinary, non-ghostly access to the house.

"No. It's all right. I've got to get over myself sometime. Besides," I reached for my margarita but diverted to my water at the last minute, "maybe nothing'll manifest if I'm not alone in the house. After all, we don't know what the trigger was. Heck, maybe it was Gil. I mean, the house was pristine. Maybe the Force objected to cat fur contaminating every available horizontal surface."

"I still can't figure out how the house *was* so clean," Ricky said, reaching for the last tortilla chip. "If Taryn didn't hire a service—"

"I didn't."

"—then it should have collected a decade's worth of dust, let alone spiders and rodents."

"Ugh." I shivered. "Don't say rodents."

He shrugged. "Sorry. But you know what I mean."

I sighed. "I do." I shifted to one hip and reached for my wallet. "What's my share of dinner?"

Ricky held up both hands. "This one's on the house for both of you."

"I can't let you—"

"My family's restaurant. My treat."

Taryn favored me with a crooked smile. "Don't bother arguing with him. You won't win."

Heat rushed up my neck because it went against the principles my parents had drilled into me from childhood—*pay your own way; don't be beholden; don't take advantage*—but I really didn't have the cash to spare.

"Thank you. I really appreciate it." I scooted to the edge of the banquette and pushed myself to my feet. "But now, I should go home. I don't want to leave Gil alone for too long."

"Afraid he'll get spooked by the spirits?" Taryn asked with a smirk.

I glared at her. "No. I'm afraid he'll scare them away and your dad will never forgive me."

She laughed, but I wasn't entirely kidding. Gil was a force of nature.

"Can I walk you home?" Ricky asked.

Tempting. So tempting. But I was trying to make *good* choices for once in my life. "I'll be fine. Thanks, though."

I lifted my hand in farewell to Ricky's family—his sister behind the bar, his mother pushing through the kitchen door with two sizzling platters of fajitas, and his father visible through the pass-through into the kitchen—and stepped out into the twilight.

Ghost's Main Street was lined with brick storefronts, its sidewalks protected by striped awnings. There were honest-to-goodness parking meters along the curb, but they were all marked *Donations only*. There were also shorter metal posts with iron rings hanging from their tops, from the days when the regular mode of transportation had been horses.

I ambled down the street, the chilly breeze teasing my curls, smiling when I noted the needlework-and-occult shop, its window displays a mix of crystals, yarn, candles, and a variety of pointy things from knitting needles to athames. It was closed for the evening, as was a bakery, unfortunately, although music drifted out of the pub across from Taqueria Vargas. On the corner, set back behind a white picket fence, was the Ghost Public Library. I peered at its sign in a neat patch of grass. Its hours were listed as Tuesday afternoon, all day Saturday, and *By Appointment*.

I shoved my hands in the pockets of my fleece jacket as I crossed Main Street and headed down Iris Lane toward the house. Somehow, I wasn't sure I could actually claim it as *mine* anymore.

Did I even want to?

I stood on the sidewalk, gazing up at it. The turrets, the gingerbread trim, the gables, the pristine spindlework. Did it hold secrets? Undoubtedly. But although most of its many windows were dark now, the house didn't seem angry or threatening or *ominous*. It seemed… lonely.

I could relate.

And despite last night's events, I still loved the place. If the vandalism was caused by humans, I'd figure it out and stop them. My retired detective client's book had a *lot* of ideas for trapping criminals.

If the house truly was haunted? Well, Gil and I would just have to learn to cohabit with a ghost.

"Although I'd really rather it would stop trashing the books," I muttered as I stalked up the flagstone walkway, digging my key out of my jeans pocket.

I squinted in the amber glow of the porch light as I aimed the key at the lock, but when I tried to insert it—

"What the—"

I crouched down and peered into the keyhole, and even in the dim light I could tell that it was once more packed with what looked like sawdust.

"Are you *kidding* me?"

Heck, the lock had been clear when I left to meet Taryn and Ricky for dinner. I'd only been gone a couple of hours, for cripes' sake. No way could mason bees mount a nesting campaign so quickly.

Wait. Could they? What did I know? Nobody'd ever hired me to ghostwrite a book about native Oregon pollinators.

I stormed down the porch steps and rounded the corner of the house. When I spotted Professor DeHaven's spectacles gleaming in her window, I eased back on my scowl and waved at her on my way to the keypad next to the garage door. Ricky had showed me how to reprogram it, so I punched in the code and crossed my arms, smirking in satisfaction as the door trundled up.

"Ha! Take that!"

I marched into the garage, giving my Civic a pat on my way past, and slapped the button to close the door. Since I didn't want Gil to dart out into the darkness, I waited for it to shut all the way before I opened the kitchen door and stepped inside.

I'd left the lights on over the kitchen counter, as well as the hall light, the light on the second floor landing, and the lamp on the library desk. Hey, don't judge or report me to the utility police. Whether my nocturnal visitors had been physical or phantasmagorical, I still didn't want to come home to a dark house.

I shrugged out of my jacket and hung it on the back of a chair in the breakfast nook as Gil came trotting in from the hallway. "Hey, boy." I picked him up and cuddled him under my chin as I considered what to do with the rest of my evening.

I was grateful for the gig Taryn had scored for me with her dad at the Manor, but with the state of my finances, I really couldn't afford to turn down any work right now.

"What do you think, Gil?" I looked down at him and he touched my nose with his. "Maybe that boring memoir isn't as bad as I recall."

I hadn't completely refused the job. Yet. I could take a look at the sample pages the prospective client sent me tonight and decide whether I could face it.

What I couldn't face, however, was working at the desk in the library, the epicenter of last night's… events. I didn't want to go up to the sitting area in my bedroom, either. In fact, I might sleep on the family room sofa tonight. You know. Just in case.

I retrieved my laptop bag from where I'd hung it on a hook by the front door and settled down at the breakfast table. I closed the blinds. Although the backyard looked quite lovely in the light from the full moon, I didn't fancy looking up to find my burglar—or something worse—staring in at me from the porch.

I booted up the laptop and opened the client's file. "Oh, lord, Gil," I muttered, "it's actually *worse* than I remember."

I scrolled down. Maybe it got better. Not everyone knew how to craft a good opening hook. But page after page was just as—

"Drivel."

My hand froze on the keyboard. I hadn't said that, and as brilliant as Gil was, he hadn't mastered human speech. I turned slowly in the chair, wishing for my trusty poker.

A man stood behind the chair, peering down at the screen. He was tall—at least as tall as me, I'd guess—and slender, although his shapeless cardigan hid much of his physique. He had a shock of curly brown hair and pale skin, with wire-framed spectacles perched on his rather hooked nose.

He was also completely transparent.

Chapter Ten

I struggled out of the chair and backed away until my hip banged into the corner of the counter. "Who… What…"

The transparent guy—okay, I guess I could say it.

The ghost.

The ghost pointed at the screen. "Did you write this?"

"N-n-no?"

He straightened, folding his arms over his chest. "Did you write it or not?"

His voice had a breathy quality, but I didn't think it was because he was trying to be flirty. In fact, his tone was decidedly severe. But it was as though he were speaking through some kind of filter or obstruction. The vocal equivalent of gauze over a camera lens.

"I didn't," I croaked. "I was just trying to decide whether to accept the job to rewrite it."

He glanced down at the screen. "Don't bother. It's not salvageable."

"I'd actually, um, come to that deci—"

Wait a minute. Why was discussing this stupid project with a ghost? Weren't there more pertinent questions to ask?

"Who are you? And why are you in my house?"

Unfortunately, we both asked exactly the same questions simultaneously.

"Your house?" Simultaneous again. "This is *my* house." And we might as well sign up for a hockey chorus because that made it a hat trick.

I edged further away, glancing around wildly for Gil. He was sitting next to the table, his fluffy tail wrapped around his feet, gazing up at the transparent guy. Considering he'd never come near Greg without the fur on his back erect like a ginger stegosaurus, that either meant the transparent guy—was I *really* going to accept he was a ghost?—was either not threatening, or else Gil was a terrible judge of character.

Then again, he'd been right about Greg.

Nevertheless, I didn't want to take a chance. I darted forward and scooped Gil up, then backed away. What was a safe distance? How fast could the transparent guy—okay, okay, *the ghost*—move? Could he just pop up wherever he liked, or did he have to walk from place to place like any non-ghost?

Jeez, there was so much I didn't know about this situation. And given that neither Saul nor Patrice, nor apparently anybody else in Ghost, had ever had a close encounter like this, it's not like I could contact them for advice. They'd be just as clueless as I was.

I gave myself a mental facepalm. *Why not ask the real expert, Maz? AKA, the one who's standing right in front of you.*

"So. Are you a ghost?"

He glared at me. "Are you?"

"No!"

"How do you know?" His tone was a combination of belligerence and what sounded like dread.

"Because… Because…" Okay, how *did* you prove you were alive and not a margarita-induced hallucination, which I still wasn't sure this guy wasn't? "Because I have a cat. I drive a car. I have past due bills. I have an ex-boyfriend who wouldn't be able to torment me with his passive-aggressive behavior if I were a ghost. Only somebody who's alive can have this much bad luck."

He snorted a laugh. "I wouldn't be too sure about that."

"So, who—"

The doorbell rang. I glanced over my shoulder. From where I stood, I could see the front door, and through the wavery glass of its half-moon light, a pair of dark eyes topped by a shock of smooth dark hair. *Ricky. Thank goodness.*

I jerked a thumb toward the foyer. "I'll just, um, get that."

The ghost shrugged, and then turned back to my laptop, his lips twisting in a sneer as he read. And yeah, couldn't blame him for that.

I scuttled toward the door, a complaining Gil tucked under my arm, and flung it open, perhaps with a little too much force.

Ricky's eyes widened and he took a step back. "Hi. Is this a bad time?"

I glanced back through the family room. The judgmental ghost was still sneering at my laptop. "Jury's kinda still out on that."

"I wanted to make sure you got home okay." He smiled diffidently, his hands tucked in the pockets of his Wranglers. "You had quite a few margaritas."

"We all did."

He chuckled. "That's true, I guess." His shoulders hunched a little. "I wanted to ask you something. You mentioned an ex-boyfriend."

"Yeah," I said slowly. "What about him?"

His tongue darted out and he licked his lips. "Are you seeing anybody now?"

I glanced over my shoulder again. *Ghost still there.* "You could say that."

His shoulders fell. "Oh. Well. That's cool. I just—"

"Do you want to come in?" I blurted.

My 180 must have startled him because he blinked. "But if you're already seeing somebody—"

"It's not like that. And I have, er, a question. About the house."

He studied me, eyebrows bunched. "Oookay." But he stepped inside. As he passed me, Gil pushed against my chest and lunged at him. Rickey caught him effortlessly. "Hey, Gil."

I led the way to the kitchen, accompanied by Gil's bone-rattling purr. The ghost was frowning at my laptop, paying zero attention to us. I pointed at him. "What's up with that?"

Ricky set Gil down, much to the cat's annoyance. "The window shades? I know they're a little outdated—"

"No, not the shades."

"The table? If you want to expand it, I can show you where the leaf is."

"No, not the table." I threaded my hands through my hair. "Isn't there anything odd about this scenario?"

He scrunched up his face in confusion, which was frankly adorable. "You mean your laptop?"

"Yes." I thrust my palms outward in a *ta da* gesture. "Exactly. *Thank* you."

"I understand if you're uncomfortable working at the desk in the library, but there's a workspace in the main bedroom, too."

My hands were suddenly too heavy to hold up, and I let my arms drop. *He can't see the ghost.* "Right."

"There's another in the bedroom in the opposite turret if you'd rather keep your work and living areas separate. I think Oren was planning to use that as his office."

The ghost's head shot up, and the look on his face—yikes. Devastation? Fury? Longing? All of the above? I braced myself for him to rush us, but instead, he disappeared. I guess that answered the transport question—unless he was still there and just invisible, which was… creepy.

I sighed. "Yeah. I've got to admit I was a little freaked about working in there, with my back to the room." I smiled weakly. "Thanks for the advice."

"No problem. So…" He peered at me from under his brows, his brown cheeks tinged with pink. "Since you're not really seeing anyone, would you like to maybe grab dinner with me sometime?" He grimaced. "Just the two of us, I mean. And maybe not in a restaurant with my family checking us out every minute."

My smile widened. "I'd like that."

"Really?" His whole face seemed to glow. "That's great. That's— How about tomorrow?"

I had to laugh. He really was adorable. Granted, we didn't exactly know one another, but I didn't think he was punking me with the ghost stuff anymore, considering I'd seen evidence to the contrary. More or less. But that's what dating was for, right?

"I'm not sure what tomorrow will look like. I'm starting work at the Manor in the morning, and until I can get an idea of the scope, I'm not sure what my schedule will be like. Maybe check in at around four? See where I'm at? Unless that's not enough time or—"

"No! No, that's fine." He held out one square, capable hand. "Want me to put my contact info in your phone?"

"Sure." I pulled it out of my pocket and handed it over. We did the whole contact-text-contact routine. "And thanks for your help with the locks..." *Right. The locks.* "You know, when I got home and tried to unlock the door, the keyhole was stuffed with sawdust again. It was only the fact you'd showed me how to reprogram the garage door that I was able to get inside."

His brows shot up. "Really? That's... Well, I won't say impossible because weirder things can happen, but highly improbable. It's a little off the mason bee life cycle for this area, and their nest detritus isn't technically sawdust, anyway."

"Okay, so sawdust-like. What else could do that?"

"Not sure. Termites and carpenter ants both affect wood, but their damage wouldn't be so localized, and they wouldn't be interested in the metal lock mechanism."

Termites. Ugh. I hated to think of my house under siege by insects as well as specters. "Do you think that's likely?"

"Not really. Besides, I check for insect damage on this place every year when I look over Tia Sofia's house and I've never seen any indication." He gestured to the door. "Mind if I take a look?"

"Be my guest."

I followed him to the door and caught Gil up when Ricky opened it and knelt to check out the lock.

"You're right. It's blocked again." He rose. "I've got my toolbox outside in my truck, though, so I'll make sure both locks are clear tonight. That okay? Shouldn't take me long."

"That would be great. Thanks." We stood there for a moment, grinning at one another, and for an instant, I thought he might lean close enough for a kiss. But instead, he raised one hand and slipped outside, leaving the door slightly ajar behind him.

I sat on the stairs again, earning myself a lapful of Gil. I sighed as I petted him, listening to Ricky humming in counterpoint to his tools.

"Is this a bad idea, Gil? I don't have the greatest track record with men. And this is a small town. If it doesn't work out, things could get… *awkward*."

On the other hand, things could turn out great. I really needed to stop sabotaging myself, even in my head. Yeah, Greg had been a mistake. And so had Neal before him, and Terry before that. But my luck had to turn sometime, right? After all, I had a home now, so why not a boyfriend?

My hands stilled on Gil's back and he nudged my arm with his nose to get them moving again. Yes, I had a home. But my home came with a judgmental ghost. A judgmental ghost whom apparently my cat and I could see, but Ricky could not.

I needed information from somebody with more experience. But where did you find somebody with actual expertise as opposed to a scam artist looking to take advantage of grieving people desperate to contact departed loved ones?

Well, my situation was slightly different: I *didn't* want to contact a loved one. I wasn't sure what I wanted, but it wasn't waking up, never knowing if my home had been trashed overnight from ghost diva fits.

I pulled out my phone and did a web search for *ghosts, banishing of*. Page after page of alleged paranormal investigators, a couple of sketchy fundamentalist exorcists, and wait…

Marguerite Windflower, Psychic Counselor.

She had a twenty-four-hour emergency number. What was the worst that could happen? Based on her website, she was located in Sarasota, so it's not like she could show up on my doorstep or send the clairvoyant cops after me. I hoped.

So I took a deep breath and dialed the number.

Chapter Eleven

"Greetings, pilgrim," said a plummy voice, backed by ethereal music that sounded like whale song accompanied by a theremin. "If you're calling about crystals or candles, please visit the online store. If you're looking for wind chimes, I'm sorry, but I no longer carry them. For custom mantras or chakra evaluation, press 1. To schedule a video session without exorcism, press 2. For a video session *with* exorcism, press 3. For all other inquiries, press 4, but if you tried raising a demon, on your own head be it. You were warned."

I pressed 4, half expecting to get another automated menu. Instead, a cheese-grater voice said, "Whatcha got?"

"Hi. Um… Sorry? Is this Marguerite Windflower?"

"The same. But Hootie says you don't need the woo-woo bullshit, so might as well get real right out of the gate. You can call me Peg."

"Okay. Yes. Well…" I took another breath. Admitting to a stranger that I'd seen a ghost was harder than I expected. "My name's Maz. Do you know anything about ghosts?"

She chuckled. "You could say that. One's been my constant companion for more years that I want to count."

"Oh thank goodness," I breathed.

"Honey, you wouldn't say that if you knew Hootie. Sucker cheats at cards. Now, what can I do for you?"

"I inherited a house out in Ghost—"

"Oregon?"

"Yes. You know it?"

"Sure. That place is haunted as shit."

I frowned, which probably came through in my tone. "But the people who live here say there's never been a manifestation."

"That's because that bonehead, Thaddeus Richdale, pissed off every spirit within a hundred-mile radius. Ghosts can carry a grudge for a long-ass time, seeing as they're not bound by details like mortality. You saying there's finally been a sighting? Where? At the Manor? That's the last place I'd expect something to happen, not with that lousy seance room smack in the middle of it, disrupting the etheric resonance."

"No. Not there. At… at my house. It's across the road from the estate."

"Hmmm." I heard the sound of a match striking. "Sounds like someone's thumbing their nose at old Richdale, doesn't it? On his very doorstep yet not crossing the threshold. The ghostly equivalent of egging his house."

"To tell you the truth, I'm not sure it has anything to do with Richdale."

"Sweetheart, in Ghost, *everything* comes back to Richdale, one way or another. But never mind him. What happened?"

I told her about the library and about the typewriter message. She whistled.

"Both gross and fine psychokinetic force *plus* unambiguous direct writing? Holy shit, kid, you've hit the trifecta."

"I don't know about the unambiguous part," I grumbled. "So, um, what does it mean when you actually *see* a ghost? I mean a transparent entity."

"Physical manifestation?" Her words were muffled, probably because she was speaking around a cigarette clenched in her teeth, but her excitement was evident. "Amorphous mist or discernable orbs?"

"Neither."

"Flashing lights? Unexplained shadows?"

"Nope. He looked like any guy at a coffee shop or the grocery. Except I could see through him."

She sucked in a breath and started coughing, so it was a while before she wheezed, "You mean a full body apparition?"

"I guess? If that means there was a transparent guy in my kitchen, making rude comments about a manuscript. Not that I could blame him. The manuscript sucked."

"Wait a minute, wait a minute. He *spoke* to you?"

"Yeah. Why? Is that unusual? Doesn't your ghost, uh, speak?"

"Speak, yes, although only to me and not with actual words. He can manipulate objects too, but he's never been visible, not even to me. Has anybody else seen this ghost?"

"My cat seems to be able to detect him. But a friend came over while the ghost was, um, commenting on the document, and he didn't spot anything unusual. Why can I see him but he couldn't?"

"Hard to tell. Could be several reasons. Maybe he considers you a kindred spirit. Maybe he thinks you can do something for him. Maybe you're simply in a place he considers his."

"Well, he did say it was his house."

"That might do it. Territoriality. Confluence of ownership."

"But why do ghosts show up in the first place?"

"Again, several reasons. Although in my experience, they're all motivated by some major life event. Something that they need or want to do. Something that left a big enough impact on their soul that they couldn't quite sever themselves from life."

"Unfinished business?" I said dryly.

"Hey, don't knock it. It's right up there in the top ten. But from what I've learned—Hootie being a case in point—they can pick up new reasons to remain on this plane. Just because they check one thing off their cosmic to-do list, doesn't mean they can't replace it with something else. In Hootie's case, it's a poker addiction and a terrible busybody tendency. He's too nosy to move on."

"Can you, well, *encourage* one to move on? And where do they move on *to*?"

"Yes to the first, although there are consequences you might not like, and as for the second? Nobody knows. As far as I've heard, once they move on, they never come back to tell us what's out there waiting."

"Say I did want to *encourage* this guy to move on. How would I go about it?"

"Well, since he can communicate with you— Is he there now, by the way?"

"No. He vanished a while back, when my friend was here."

"Once he comes back, ask him."

"Ask him what?"

"Who he is. What he wants. What would make him happy."

"Make him happy? How the heck do you make a ghost happy?"

"*I* don't know," she said, exasperation clear in her tone. "That's why you *ask*. Don't complain, pal. You've got a huge advantage. Most people who are haunted just have to guess."

I sighed. "Okay. Is there, um, any danger? I mean, he was able to throw books around. Could he hurt me? Hurt my cat?"

She hummed tunelessly, obviously thinking. "Can't rule it out. Most injuries are more collateral damage—like if you'd been standing in the way of one of the books. But your guy is already high on the haunting scale, so ordinary rules may not apply. Might be a good idea to keep a go-bag ready. Just in case."

"Thanks. That's so comforting."

"Hey. I don't make this shit up. Ghost still has that occult shop on Main Street, right?"

"Sort of, although it's merged with a needlework store."

"Then give me your email and I'll send you some info on protective herbs and crystals."

"Okay." I gave it to her. "And thanks. Really. What do I owe you for the consult?"

"Don't worry about it. This one's on the house. Good luck, kid. Keep in touch. I want to hear how things turn out."

I disconnected the call and sighed. "Just ask him," I muttered to Gil. "Like that's so easy. I don't know when he'll show up again."

However, I decided to take Marguerite's—*Peg's*—advice and prepare for a quick bug-out. It wasn't like I'd actually be able to sleep tonight, not when I was wondering when that transparent guy might pop in and peer at me from the ceiling like River Tam in *Serenity*.

So I prioritized my most precious possessions: to wit, Gil and my laptop. I loaded Gil into his carrier with a few treats. He complained a bit, but settled down to snooze after gobbling the treats. I tucked my laptop into my messenger bag and slung it over my shoulder. Then I sat down at the table, my car keys clutched in my hand, and waited.

And waited.

And waited.

And *waited*.

After about half an hour, the keys had made painful ridges in my palms and my shoulder itched under the bag's strap. Clearly I needed a better strategy.

I uncurled my cramped fingers and set the keys on the table to shake out my hand. Transparent guy had shown up when I'd been reviewing that awful memoir. Maybe he'd show up again for the same reason. It hadn't appeared that he could scroll the screen before, so maybe his ability to interact with the environment, so to speak, was limited to things that didn't require the touch of actual skin.

I set the laptop up again and opened the document. I waited for another ten minutes, and when still nothing happened, I decided to escalate. I scrolled down to the beginning of the second chapter and cleared my throat.

"'On my second day of first grade, my Superman lunchbox held an apple, a bologna sandwich on Wonder Bread with mayonnaise, two Chips Ahoy! cookies, and a box of Capri Sun cranberry apple juice. I sat next to Sherman Dudikoff on the bus. He was wearing a red T-shirt to my green plaid button-down although both had short sleeves since the weather report predicted the temperature would rise above seventy-two degrees by recess. When we reached the school, he—'"

"Drivel."

I took a breath, turned slowly, and yep. He was back, once more glaring at the screen.

I swallowed hard, because this was it. *Talking to a ghost.* "Yes. It is."

He tore his gaze from the train wreck of a memoir and focused on me, which was really weird, because while I could tell his eyes behind his spectacles were dark and intense, I could see the kitchen cabinets through them. "Then why are you reading it?"

"I'm trying to decide whether to take the job of vetting it."

He straightened. "Don't. It's hopeless."

"I've come to the same conclusion, however, I need the work." I stood up slowly, so he wouldn't be looming over me, and discovered we were exactly the same height. "I'm Maz Amani."

"I don't know any Maz Amani."

"You do now." I swallowed, rubbing my damp palms along my jeans. "Who are you?"

His forehead wrinkled, as though he were confused by the question. "I live here." He glanced around. "This is my home."

I felt like a total bonehead when the light dawned. "You're Avi."

His frown deepened. "That's what I said." He looked around. "My home. *Our* home. It's just what we'd imagined. Just what he promised. Our place. Where we'd be together."

"Who promised?"

His confusion was clearly tempered with impatience now. "He did. Oren. Once he's finished in Toronto, he'll be back and we'll be together."

Of course. Oren. But Oren had never come back, because Avi had died.

"Oren is gone, Avi," I said gently.

"Yes, I know that." He turned and moved out of the kitchen with the slight jerkiness of somebody walking, not floating, although I wasn't certain his feet actually met the floor. "He's been gone for months on that Toronto job. But I made sure our home is ready and waiting for when he gets back." I caught up with him outside the library and he smiled a little shyly. "I haven't even slept in the new bed yet. I wanted the first time to be with him."

"That's not what I—" *Dial it back, Maz. Don't, er, spook him.* "Avi, what year is it?"

"That's a stupid question."

"Well, I'm the guy who's considering vetting that manuscript, so humor me. What year is it?"

"2014."

"No. It's not. It's 2024. And I'm here because this is my house now. I inherited it from my Uncle Oren."

He stilled. "You can't. You couldn't have. You can only inherit something if somebody is… If they're…"

His eyes, wide, dark, and yep, transparent, begged me to tell him something other than what I was about to. I bit my lip and spread my hands, palms up, because he didn't really need me to say the words. He knew what I meant.

Silvery tears spilled over his lashes and tracked down his face. Behind him, through the library doors, I spotted Professor DeHaven's neat stack of *Borderline* pages beginning to flutter on the desk.

"Uh oh," I muttered.

A moment later, a book toppled off a shelf, followed by two more on the other side of the room. I really didn't want this to escalate into another library tornado, so I lunged forward, reaching for him. But he choked out a sob and disappeared.

After he vanished, I stayed where I was outside the library doors, well out of the way of any books that might suddenly take flight. But the papers on the desk settled, and nothing else became airborne.

What were the chances Avi was done for the night? He hadn't seemed angry or hostile to me specifically. Only sad. So I decided to roll with it and take a chance. I needed to be sharp tomorrow if I wanted to impress Saul and justify Taryn's contract terms, and for that, I needed sleep.

I collected Gil in his carrier and headed upstairs. "Hope our resident ghost isn't a voyeur, Gil, because I really can't go another day without a proper shower."

Chapter Twelve

My hips complained strongly about sleeping on the floor a second night running, but after Avi's remarks about saving the bed for his and Oren's first night in the house, I didn't want to take the chance that might trigger him. Yeah, there were other beds, but I wanted to keep my footprint in the house as small as possible, at least until Avi and I had another chat or two and I had a chance to ask him what would make him happy.

Unfortunately, I suspected I was completely incapable of providing what would truly make him happy: Oren.

I took a shower in the bathroom in the hallway, which seemed to have the fewest personal touches. No ghost stuck his head through the door, so I counted that as a win, but it was still one of the shortest showers of my life.

I shook out my curls—I'd learned early in life not to comb or brush them unless I wanted to resemble a tumbleweed—and dressed in my least-worn black jeans and a dusty blue pinstripe button-up, which was about as formal as my clothes went at the moment. When you worked from home in a practically invisible job, you didn't have a lot of occasions to go out on the town. Which was another thing Greg objected to, along with my composure in the face of his escalating efforts to provoke an argument: *"My gawd, Maz, can't you see how* serious *this is?"*

He broke that one out for any topic from our precarious relationship to the lack of almond milk in the fridge. *"What will it take to get you to* engage *for once in your life?"*

I couldn't help that—my mom had also been relentlessly calm, claiming that panic never solved anything but to breed more panic.

"Congratulations, Greg, and sorry, Mom," I muttered to my reflection. "I'm living in a haunted house. I might have finally found something that'll push me over the edge."

Gil watched me tame my scruff with my beard trimmer from his perch on the counter next to the sink with his usual judgmental expression, occasionally licking a paw and swiping it over his ear as if to show me his clearly superior grooming method.

Crap. Gil.

Even though he didn't seem unduly disturbed by Avi's presence, I didn't know if the reverse was also true. I couldn't leave him alone in the house, not until I was certain he'd be safe. However, I couldn't inflict Gil on the Manor, even if Saul understood the reason for my worry, because the museum was a public place. If any visitors were allergic to cats, it would be a problem.

He batted the water as I rinsed off the trimmer and weighed my options. Ricky's Tia Sofia had seemed to like Gil, and—what was more important—he seemed to like her. Would she be willing to cat-sit for me? Couldn't hurt to ask, as long as I made sure to emphasize that *no* was a perfectly okay response.

"Come on, big guy." I turned off the water and scooped him up. "Let's see if our neighbor is willing to put you up for the day."

I put him back in his carrier—earning a glare before he circled around to present his very judgmental butt. "Yeah, yeah. I know. But it's for your own good."

His tail twitched twice. He never believed me when I said that about the vet, either.

I crept downstairs, peering into the library from the landing. It didn't *seem* like any other literature had launched itself overnight. I scuttled down the rest of the stairs and through the family room, where all the throw pillows were neatly in place. The kitchen, too, was just as pristine as it was last night. Except…

I set Gil's carrier down and edged toward the counter, where a single piece of white paper lay. The hair on my neck prickled, because the paper contained one typed word:

sorry

I cleared my throat. "It's okay. But if, you know, you're the one who's been stuffing the keyholes with sawdust? I'd really appreciate it if maybe you could not do that today?"

I waited, my gaze darting around the room, but nobody appeared and nothing moved. I wasn't sure whether that constituted agreement, or whether I'd just been talking to myself.

I pocketed my keys, and as I stowed my laptop in my messenger bag, my gaze caught on the paper once more. Saul and Professor DeHaven would probably swoon with this evidence, along with details about my chat with Avi, so before I could second-guess myself, I carefully slid the page into the outside pocket of the bag. They'd probably have preferred to see it *in situ,* but it was just lying on the counter, something I—or anybody else—could have done.

I glanced over my shoulder as the phantom spiders returned for their daily Zumba warmup. A ghost was one thing. But this house was really big. Could there be secret passages? Crawlspaces? Gaps in the walls? I'd heard stories about intruders living inside their victims' house for *months* before going on a rampage. But the house was quiet except for the hum of the big refrigerator. And it had been empty when I arrived. Could someone live in a house undetected without leaving any trace?

"You know what, Gil? I think I prefer the ghost, so let's go with that, huh? You're still not staying here alone, though."

I grabbed the reusable bag with Gil's cat food and toys, and my hand was on the garage door handle when my doorbell rang. I checked my watch: 7:30. Who went calling at this hour?

Like, for instance, I'd been about to do to Sofia.

"Talk about glass houses," I muttered as I schlepped down the hall, messenger bag, cat carrier and all. I perked up a little when I spotted Ricky through the glass.

I opened the door with a smile I couldn't suppress. "Hey."

His smile faded a little when he saw my all my luggage. "Are you leaving?"

"What? Oh, no." I chuckled and patted my messenger bag. "Just heading over to the Manor to start my new gig."

He lifted one eyebrow. "Does Gil assist you in your work?"

I huffed a laugh. "No. But given the, uh, *events* here yesterday, I didn't feel comfortable leaving him on his own here. As a matter of fact, I was planning to ask your Tia Sofia if she'd mind if he hung out with her today. But then I realized it's a little A) last minute and B) early to impose."

Ricky grinned and held out his hand for Gil's carrier. "Not at all. She'll be delighted. She hasn't had a cat since she lost hers about five years ago." He shook his head. "Princesa lived to the ripe old age of twenty-two and was pampered every single day."

"Why didn't she get another one?" I asked as I passed Gil over.

His smile faded under an expression of disgust. "Liam."

"Who's Liam?"

"Her grandson.

"She has another one? She mentioned Guillermo, but—"

"That's Liam. He decided Guillermo was too *ethnic* and started insisting everybody call him Liam back in high school. He *claims* to be allergic to cats, which is the excuse he gives for not visiting Tia Sofia more often—or at all, since he left for college."

"If her cat's been gone for five years, though—"

"What can I say? The guy's a tool. But Tia won't hear a word against him. Still thinks he hung the moon." He patted Gil's carrier. "She'll be thrilled for Gil's company, trust me. I was heading over there anyway, so I can drop him off."

"Thank you. Really." I handed him the bag. "These are his essentials. I've got a spare litter pan too, if—"

"No need. She still has Princesa's stuff. She never could face giving it away."

I studied him, my head to one side. "Somehow, I don't imagine you stopped by this morning because your super-secret ESP powers told you I needed a babysitter for my cat."

That rosy pink glowed along his cheekbones again. He set the carrier down and retrieved a blue and white striped paper bag from beside the door. "No. I, um, just wanted to give you this. I wasn't sure you'd be up, so I was just going to leave it, but then I saw you through the window, and, well…"

Warmth sprouted under my heart as I took the bag. "What's this?" I opened it up and the heavenly aroma of cinnamon and nutmeg wafted out. I peeked inside to see a plump, golden brown muffin resting in a nest of tissue paper. "Wow."

"Isaksen's signature pumpkin spice muffin." He dropped his gaze and scuffed the toe of one Converse along the whitewashed porch decking. "For your first day. I figured it would either be for luck before you started or a reward for making it through, so you'd have something good to snack on, even if you don't have time for dinner tonight."

Okay, can I say my heart melted? Because my heart melted. Heck, Greg had never brought me breakfast. Or lunch. Or a freaking takeout dinner, for that matter. That had always been *my* job—*"Because I have to go to the office and you're at home all day."*

I was home all day *working,* so going out was actually an interruption when he could easily grab something on his way home, but that's not how he saw it.

"This is fantastic. Thank you. Truly." I leaned forward to kiss his cheek.

News flash: It was just as smooth and warm as it looked.

He ducked his head and… was that a giggle? Whatever, it was ridiculously cute. "Have a good day." He stooped to pick up Gil's carrier. "And don't worry about him. Tia will dote on him."

"Uh oh. He probably won't want to come home with me then." I raised a hand in farewell as he walked down the porch stairs. "I'll call you about dinner."

"Great. Talk to you then." He turned and actually skipped a couple of steps as he crossed the lawn toward Sofia's house.

Seriously. *So* cute.

I ducked back inside—making sure the door was locked—and made my way through the house to the garage, mentally kicking my butt all the way.

Yes, he was cute. And nice. But could I really impose my baggage on a nice, cute guy? Greg had always cited my failed relationships: *"What's the common denominator here, Maz? You!"* He'd claimed I was selfish and emotionally unavailable—usually when I was in the middle of my work day, or when he'd made another stab at getting me to ghostwrite his ridiculous espionage thriller.

Here in this new town, I might have a chance to remake my image, but I still couldn't categorize myself as much of a catch: Recently homeless. Mostly unemployed. And oh yeah—living in a haunted house.

"Who wouldn't want to sign up for that?" I muttered as I slapped the garage door opener. I slid into the Civic and set my bag on the passenger seat, where the foam stuffing was peeking out from the split upholstery. I'd found the remote opener in a basket on the workbench that lined one side of the garage, so at least I could close the door behind me without climbing out and entering the code.

I'd decided to drive to the Manor the first day because I wasn't sure how far it actually was to the doors. Saul had told me to follow the fence along Main Street to the first right, so I did, nibbling on the truly fantastic muffin along the way.

Making the turn onto Violet Road, I wondered briefly whether all the roads in Ghost were named after flowers. The Manor's iron gates—thankfully wide open—were at least a quarter of a mile from the corner, and once I passed through, the gravel driveway snaked through the trees for at least another quarter of a mile. When the Manor finally came into view, I had to brake for a moment, because *wow.*

I'd thought my house was big, but this place was *huge.*

"No wonder he called it a manor," I murmured.

My house had two turrets. This one had at least five that I could see, red-shingled with decorative metal toppers that seemed too short to be lightning rods, but its massive facade was clearly the tip of the Victorian iceberg.

There was at least an acre of grass—a little shaggy and dotted with the occasional dandelion—sweeping from the drive to a boxy hedge that framed a fountain circled by four marble statues. The wide porch that spanned the front of the mansion was backed by tall windows, ensuring very nice views of the statues' bare backsides, and the massive front doors were *juuust* off-center enough to look unsettling.

A big wooden sign in the same style as the one in front of the library stood at the edge of the lawn. It read *Richdale Manor* in giant gilt letters, and underneath in smaller font, *Museum and Gift Shop.* A more discreet sign attached to its bottom by black chains directed me to *Parking,* so I followed the arrows for *another* quarter mile—jeez, the footprint of this place had to be bigger than the entire town—and swung into the gravel lot that was at least as big as my back yard, Professor DeHaven's, and Sofia's put together.

And totally empty, except for a single dusty Nissan LEAF.

Chapter Thirteen

As I parked next to the lone car, I hoped the absence of visitors was because of the early hour and not lack of tourist interest. Given Taryn's comments, though, I suspected the Manor was having as much trouble attracting tourist dollars as the town of Ghost as a whole.

I finished the last bite of muffin and climbed out of my car, brushing crumbs off my jeans, and slung my messenger bag over my shoulder. Locking up was irrelevant. For one thing, if anybody was desperate enough to steal the Civic, they had more problems than I did. For another... Did I mention the fenced grounds, long driveway, and empty parking lot?

I stood next to the car for a minute, uncertain how to get in. But just as I'd finally decided to circle around to the front verandah, Saul poked his head out a door near the rear of the house. I hadn't noticed it because it was camouflaged by an odd combination of shadows and weird wall angles. In fact, even though I'd seen it now, I wasn't sure I'd be able to spot it again if it was closed.

"Maz! Good to see you!" Saul beckoned me over. "Come in this way."

When I jogged over to meet him, he held the door for me and gestured for me to enter. I stepped inside what was clearly a visitor's center—complete with a ticket window, spinners of postcards, and shelves of merchandise, although the merch was a little sparse.

"Good morning."

"So glad you could make it." Saul led me through the room and into a hallway. He tapped the wallpaper above the cream-painted shiplap wainscoting. "Thaddeus had this wallpaper custom made to honor his daughters."

I peered at the delicate floral designs on the ivory background. "I take it his daughters were named Daisy, Violet, and Iris?"

"Daisy, Violet, Iris… and Caroline."

My eyebrows shot up. "That seems… pointed."

Saul shrugged. "Apparently Frances, Thaddeus's wife, put her foot down when he wanted to name the fourth girl Heliotrope."

"And I'm sure Caroline was grateful."

"That's undetermined. From all accounts, Caroline was the least… compliant of the Richdale children, possibly because other than her twin, Cornelius—"

"Cornelius? Really? Why do people persist in giving twins alliterative names? Isn't it enough they've got the same birthday? Give them their own initials, for Pete's sake."

"I suspect the alliteration was the least of her worries. Her other siblings persisted in calling her Ragweed."

I winced. "Ouch."

"Exactly." He continued down the hall, making at least three sharp right angle turns before stopping at the foot of a narrow staircase. "We'll take the servant's stairs."

"Seems appropriate."

"Yes, well, we do live to serve."

I followed him up the steps to the second floor, where he ushered me out of the stairwell and down a wide hallway into a long, light-filled room, its ceiling and paneled walls painted white, a jewel-toned rug on its gleaming hardwood floor. Judging by the ceiling angles that framed a tall, multi-paned window, we had to be in one of the many gables I'd noted from outside.

Saul grinned at my slack-jawed expression. "We may live to serve, but that doesn't mean we have to be miserable while we're doing it. Please. Have a seat." He took his place behind the massive oak desk that sat in front of the window, and I managed to stumble across the room and sit in a brocade-padded chair across from him. He rested his elbows on his chair arms and laced his fingers across his middle. "I've been intending to inventory and organize Thaddeus Richdale's papers practically since I was hired on as director."

"When was that, sir?"

He waved one hand. "Oh, please. Call me Saul. No need for formality here."

"All right. Saul, then."

"To answer your question, about five years ago. I'm a lawyer by training. Used to practice here in town. Taryn took over my practice when my husband and I decided to semi-retire." He smiled wryly. "Little did we know that we'd be working harder in retirement than if we'd stayed with our original professions."

"What does your husband do?"

"He's now the town's librarian—totally unpaid—although he used to be the only family practice doctor in Ghost. He also volunteers with adoption and surrogacy agencies, helping to place children with loving families, and to help families like our own grow and prosper. Of course, he did that before he retired too. It was his passion project. You'll find a number of families here in Ghost who owe him for his work."

"That's lovely."

His smile turned tender. "Yes. He is."

"If you don't mind my asking, why haven't you been able to make progress with the papers? Are they stored poorly or damaged?"

"Not a bit. Thaddeus was meticulous in his record-keeping because he wanted to ensure that if any of his efforts to contact the other side succeeded, he'd be able to replicate the process. He also kept diaries, as did his wife and two of his six children.

There are *crates* of the things, so if you think I was just throwing you a bone, please disabuse yourself of that notion."

"Crates?" I said faintly.

He nodded. "Crates. A whole room full of them. And the reason I haven't been able to even make a start is that all my time is taken up with fundraising to try and keep the place afloat." He grimaced. "And did I mention I'm supposed to be retired? I do try to work fewer than sixty hours a week nowadays."

"So what do you envision for the result? Do you want to just organize and catalog the papers? Cross-reference them? Scan them into digital copies?"

"All of that, yes. But what I'd really like is the story of Richdale and his quest in an entertaining and easily digestible story. Nothing dry or academic. Anecdotal. Something that visitors could pick up in the gift shop on their way out. Does that make sense?"

"Absolutely." Belatedly, I dug in my bag and pulled out a pad and pen to take notes. "The Dunsmuir estate up in Victoria has something similar."

"Exactly! Is that something you could do?"

I shifted a little uneasily. "In terms of ability, yes. I've ghostwritten similar books for clients who wanted their family stories… well, not fictionalized, but novelized?" When Saul nodded, I went on. "However, it depends a lot on the material. If the stories are there in the papers, I can pull them out and make them entertaining. But if there's nothing of interest?" I spread my hands. "I'm not a novelist. I can vet what's there, but I can't invent it from whole cloth."

He chuckled. "Oh, don't worry. The papers might be extensive, but there's a story there. Thaddeus was quite a character, and the rest of his family wasn't exactly boring. Cornelius ended up as a stuntman in silent pictures." Then he sat forward, eyes sparkling. "Now, how was your second night in your house? Did you experience any other manifestations?"

Okay, here goes. "As a matter of fact, yes." I extracted the paper from my bag and slid it across the wide polished desk. "This was on the kitchen counter this morning."

His eyes widened and he picked it up, holding it between the thumb and forefinger of each hand. "Oh," he breathed. "Not even left on the typewriter? Actually moved downstairs to the kitchen? That's *extraordinary.*"

I took a moment to wonder if Saul owned a half dozen time shares or had fallen for emails from displaced Nigerian princes, because he seemed far too innocent and trusting for a retired lawyer. If somebody had handed me that paper and said a ghost had typed it up and schlepped it downstairs, I'd have called bullshit in a heartbeat.

I knew that's exactly what had happened, but Saul had only my word for it.

"Do you suppose they're apologizing for the mess in the library?" he asked.

His voice was soft, so I wasn't entirely sure he was speaking to me, but I took a deep breath. "No. He was apologizing for almost doing it again."

Saul's head snapped up. "What?" And *there* was the lawyer voice.

I clasped my hands together in my lap. "When I was looking over the manuscript for a prospective client, someone, er, commented on it from behind my back."

His eyes widened. "They *spoke*? You *heard* them?"

"Yep. He was, um, a little judgmental about the quality of the writing."

Now his eyes narrowed. "'He'? It was a male voice?"

"Yes." I swallowed. "And not only a voice. I could see him."

Saul let go of the paper, which drifted to the desktop, and fell back in his chair. "You *saw* someone," he croaked. "An actual apparition?"

"Not only that. I know who it was." I took another breath. This might be tough for Saul to hear. It's one thing to poke around in ghost stories from Thaddeus Richdale's era, but this was someone Saul had known personally. "It was Avi."

Chapter Fourteen

Saul paled. "Avi? Avi Felder?"

I nodded. "We, um, had a chat. He wasn't aware that time had passed, and he didn't know that Oren was dead."

Saul carded his fingers through his snowy hair. "Oh my god. Poor Avi." He took a couple of shallow breaths. "Are you sure?"

I nodded. "Patrice is going to— Can we go over there now?"

"I don't think that would do any good. For one thing, he wasn't hanging around when I left. For another, I'm not sure anybody else could see him."

His gaze sharpened. "What makes you think so?"

"Ricky stopped by yesterday when Avi was, er, manifesting. He didn't see anything, didn't seem to sense anything unusual."

"But you did?"

"Yes. And I think Gil can see him too. Or at least sense that something's there." I snorted. "On the other hand, Gil's been known to stare at a knothole for hours without twitching a whisker, so I'm not sure he's the best indicator."

Saul sighed, and his gaze turned pleading. "If you see him again, would you call me? Call us both, Patrice and me? Please?"

I screwed up my face. "I guess. But once he's, well, achieved his goal, whatever it might be, he just disappears. So even if he's there when I call, he might not be there when you arrive."

"I don't care," Saul said fiercely. "Just the possibility is reason enough for the trip. Promise me, please. Any day, any time. 24/7. If he appears, call us."

"Okay." I bit my lip. "If you don't mind my asking, how exactly did Avi die? I, um, didn't want to ask him."

Saul cleared his throat and tugged on the front of his blue button-down as though settling back into himself. "Avi grew up in Ghost. In that very house, in fact."

That tied in with what Carson had told me the first day. "And Oren?" At Saul's raised eyebrows, I spread my hands, palms up. "I never met him, you know. He was my mom's second cousin once removed. I have no idea how he knew I existed, let alone why he left me the house and everything in it."

"Ah. I see." He steepled his fingers. "Oren was an architect, a partner in a firm up in Portland with a lot of national and international contracts. It was a fluke he ever came to town because usually they did much higher end projects. But the couple who'd bought the Jenkinses' dilapidated Victorian on the other side of town and wanted to turn it into a B & B were friends with one of the other partners. Oren volunteered for the project because he loved nineteenth century architecture. He and Avi ran into each other in one of the shops on Main Street and that was it for both of them, even though Avi was almost twelve years Oren's junior."

"Really? Love at first sight?"

Saul smiled sadly. "Let's say attraction at first sight. But they never passed up a chance to be together after that. Oren planned the renovations on Avi's house—your house—in his spare time. He intended to leave the Portland firm and set up his practice here once he moved in with Avi, so he was burning a lot of hours with them leading up to the split."

"Out of guilt?"

"Terms of the partnership agreement, actually." Saul turned away, blinking rapidly. "They were so happy."

"But then?"

Saul dashed a hand under his eyes. "They'd planned a big party, a combination housewarming-slash-reveal of the renovated house along with a welcome-to-town for Oren, who was supposed to have officially left the old firm that day. But Oren was held up on his last project—he'd been in Toronto for two months already—and couldn't make it."

I winced. "Ugh. Not the best way to start a new life together."

"No. Someone—I think it might have been Ricky, since he was one of the few people other than the construction crews who Avi and Oren allowed in the house..." He trailed off and met my gaze a little defiantly, as though I might be judging his friends. "The better to maintain the surprise, you understand. Anyway, Ricky overheard Avi having a very heated phone conversation with Oren a couple of days before the party, and the next day, Ricky said Avi seemed... off. Distracted. Occasionally inattentive. Not himself, anyway, but he chalked it up to whatever the argument had been about. The party went on—out in the back yard, with all their friends laughing, eating, drinking, excited about seeing the house. But then, as Avi was mounting the porch steps to usher everyone inside, he just... collapsed."

"Collapsed? Was he dehydrated? Low blood sugar? Overheated?"

"None of those. It wasn't that hot, and he'd been eating and drinking, even if not as enthusiastically as the rest of us. He hit his head on the edge of the deck as he fell, opened a gash on his forehead, but Jerry—my husband, who was still the town doctor at the time as well as the county ME—said he was dead before he fell. Subdural hematoma."

I tried to process this. "Do subdural hematomas develop spontaneously?"

"They can, although it's more likely the result of a blow of some kind. They can develop gradually, however, so it's possible he hit his head days before his death and didn't realize there was any problem." He gazed down at his laced fingers. "Oren never came back to Ghost. Never even set foot in the house. He told me he couldn't bear to be there without Avi, so I should lock up the place and he'd give me further instructions later."

"And did he?"

Saul spread his hands and shrugged. "Just updated his will to make you the sole beneficiary. He was on the deed already—Avi had put him on it when they started the renovation. And since Avi's will left everything to Oren, and Oren left everything to you..."

"I get it." I sighed. "I wish I could have known Oren. Heck, I wish I'd known he *existed*. But my parents were a pretty self-sufficient couple. They were happy with the three of us and Mom always preferred to look forward instead of back. I think she did mention once after I came out that she was glad she didn't have much to do with her extended family. They weren't very open-minded."

Saul lifted one snow-white eyebrow. "Maybe that's why he left everything to you. If the extended family was intolerant, I'd imagine he wouldn't be thrilled to enrich any of them in any way. Do you suppose he knew you were gay?"

"Maybe? It's possible my mother had some contact with him. But my folks were committed to their nomadic lifestyle by then, so there probably wasn't a lot of chance for a reunion before their accident."

"Accident?"

I swallowed against the threat of tears. "Their RV went off the road someplace in the Rockies."

"Ah. I'm sorry."

"It was a long time ago. Almost ten years, when I was still in college."

"About the time Oren lost Avi. That might be why he made you his heir. He knew what it was like to be alone."

I couldn't help the flare of indignation and, yes, anger, because seriously? My hand tightened on my pen, the clip cutting into my palm. "If that's so, why didn't he contact me then?"

Saul reached out, but the desk was too wide for him to get anywhere close to me. He sighed and let his hand drop to the blotter. "Grief is an odd thing, son. We all handle it differently. From what I've heard, Oren turned into a virtual recluse after that. Our only communication was via email or snail mail. He never spoke to anyone in town again, and although he still worked for his Portland firm, he withdrew as a partner and never met with clients again."

I rubbed my chest, trying to ease that twinge of pain at being ignored, abandoned. I knew it wasn't fair—Oren had never met me, and he'd provided for me the best he could, as my parents had been unable to do. And I understood how funky grief could be—I dropped out of school for two years and worked a series of short-term retail gigs while I processed the loss of my parents. Come to think of it, that might be why Oren couldn't find me, even if he'd looked. I'd moved around *a lot*.

"Could your husband determine anything else about Avi's accident?" I asked. Saul hesitated and I frowned. "It *was* an accident, wasn't it?"

Again, he spread his hands. "Avi was mostly alone in the house all the time by then. He was trying to finish a book—"

"The one that's still subject to a lawsuit?"

"Yes. That one. So, he was busy, working against a deadline while trying to get the house ready for Oren's arrival and the big reveal. I think Ricky, Sofia, and Patrice were the only people he'd let inside. Sofia because she cooked for him, Ricky because he was doing odd jobs and helping with the finishing details on the house."

"And Patrice?"

"She was his beta reader. He'd leave pages for her in the library for her review, but she told me later that he hadn't passed anything along for several weeks. She'd seen nothing of the latest book."

I had a very weird feeling about this. Didn't Marguerite say that ghosts tended to be motivated by significant life events?

That they could carry grudges? I'd think somebody coshing you on the head would be a pretty strong incentive to stick around and, well, stick it to them. Although so far, Avi had seemed more sad than angry or vindictive—as long as you didn't count the first library tornado.

"Do you think... That is, would your husband be willing to talk to me about Avi's death?"

"I expect he can do better than that. Let me call and have him pull his folio for you."

"Folio?"

"He's the volunteer librarian and the library doesn't get a lot of foot traffic. He spends his time collating materials on anything that interests him. And Avi's death definitely interested him." He peered at me from under his eyebrows. "He had some concerns about it, too." He picked up the handset on his desk phone. "Go on over to the library now. Thaddeus's papers will still be here when you get back."

"But it's not a Tuesday or Saturday."

Saul chuckled as he punched in the number. "Ah, but you forget. It's open by appointment too. Trust me. He'll be happy to meet with you." He flapped his free hand. "Go. Shoo. We live around the corner from the library, so he'll probably beat you there."

Who was I to argue? I shooed.

Chapter Fifteen

Jerry McHale was about as different from Saul Pasternak as he could be. He was at least three inches shy of six feet, carried a comfortable amount of padding around his middle—although it was somewhat disguised by his colorful Hawaiian shirt—and his dark hair still had more pepper than steel-gray salt. Where Saul's face was long and angular, Jerry's was full and round. One thing they had in common though—the kindness in their eyes, although Jerry's were sky blue to Saul's deep brown.

He met me on the library's front steps and shook my hand warmly. "You must be Maz. Taryn told me all about you."

I smiled crookedly. "About how many margaritas it takes before I'm under the table?"

He chuckled, a warm, welcoming sound, and I felt a pang of envy for his former patients. His bedside manner must have been epic. "Not a bit." He pulled a set of keys out of his dad-jeans pocket and unlocked the door. "I understand you're interested in the man who lived in your house."

"Both of them, actually." I followed him into an airlock-type vestibule, a pair of glass doors separating us from the library proper, with big bulletin boards on the walls to either side, although the one on the left was completely bare and the one on the right only sported a notice for somebody selling a mountain bike, a signup sheet for a book club with no takers, and a faded poster for the Ghost Halloween parade, dated over three years in the past. Jerry noticed me looking at it and sighed.

"I probably should take that down, but it's from the last time we staged the parade. A bit of nostalgia if you like."

"Why was it the last?" I asked as he led me through the doors and into the library. It wasn't a large building, but it was a decent size. Wide rather than deep, with alcoves clearly labeled for children's and YA books, as well as tables and padded chairs arranged to break up the rows of shelves. I inhaled deeply. *Damn*, I loved the smell of books.

He set the keys on the circulation counter gently, as though he didn't want to break the silence. "It was the last because nobody came."

I stopped inhaling eau de books and stared at him. "Nobody came to the parade?"

"Well, Ghost residents came. But it used to be a three-day festival. Portland has Bigfoot and Beyond. McMinnville has their UFO Fest. Ghost was trying to do something similar with Ghost Days, but interest had been waning for several years as we went longer and longer without an actual haunting."

Well, those days are gone. But I kept my mouth shut about *that* for the moment.

"First we scaled back to two days, then one, then just the parade. But when the university started staging their Oktoberfest at the same time, we lost even that small amount of interest, so we pulled the plug."

I glanced over my shoulder at the poster. It actually looked like it could be a fun event, but I thought they'd made a mistake by scaling back. They should have gone the other way and made it bigger, splashier, spookier, with or without actual spooks. But nobody had asked me and I was here for another reason.

"Mr. McHale—"

"Jerry, please. You'll find that nobody in Ghost stands on ceremony."

"Jerry, then. Saul told you why I'm here, and I hope you don't think I'm being presumptuous, but you conducted Avi Felder's autopsy, didn't you?"

He nodded. "Call it a postmortem examination rather than an autopsy. I was a backup ME with the county at the time. I wouldn't have chosen to do the exam on a friend, but there wasn't anyone else available. Plus, as Avi was Jewish, we couldn't delay before the burial. He didn't have any family living, but Oren made his wishes known."

"Saul said Oren never came back to town after Avi's death. Not even for the funeral?"

"He tried, but he couldn't get a flight. We held off on the ceremony as long as we could, but..." Jerry sighed and shook his head. "This way."

Jerry bustled over to a horseshoe-shaped desk under a suspended *Reference* sign and sat in the swivel chair behind it. He gestured to one of the rolling chairs in front of a bank of old-style VDT monitors. "Grab one of those and make yourself comfortable."

I pulled one over and settled down while he reached under the desk and pulled out a post-bound archival scrapbook that was big enough to hold an entire newspaper page.

"There's not a lot," he said, flipping carefully through the heavy black pages with their polypropylene protectors. "An account of the party. The obituary. My report, of course, wasn't released to the press." He chuckled, shaking his head. "The press. The *Boos News*, our weekly paper— Don't look at me like that. *I* didn't name it."

I dialed back my *seriously?* expression. "Sorry."

"Yes. Well. It wasn't what you'd call Pulitzer-level journalism back then, although Nitya, the new editor, is doing their best to raise the standards." He squinted at the page before muttering a curse and pulling a pair of half-moon cheaters out of his shirt pocket and perching them on his nose. "Anyway, Avi died on a Saturday and the paper publishes on Wednesday, so there's an article about the upcoming party in the previous week's issue, and the obituary and details about the event the week afterward. But I could swear there was something…" He scanned the next page, and a smile lit his face, "Aha! There it is. A letter to the editor." He glanced up at me over his glasses. "The paper doesn't get many of those, but the next month, they did. An anonymous one, at that. Hinting that Avi's death might have been the result of foul play."

I straightened in the uncomfortable chair. "Foul play? Did they say why they suspected it? Who they suspected?"

He waggled one hand. "Indirectly. Although they didn't accuse him in so many words, they did hint that Oren was the only person who materially gained from Avi's death."

I was outraged on Uncle Oren's behalf, despite having never met him. "He wasn't even here!"

"Ah." He tapped one finger on the article and leaned forward with a conspiratorial whisper. "Hit men."

I snorted a laugh, something that always made Greg roll his eyes. "Hit men? In *Ghost*?"

"Well, let's say individuals who are willing to do unsavory tasks for a price."

"That could apply to the guys who muck out stables," I muttered.

"I didn't say it was at all likely. Only that this particular correspondent—" He flipped the page, then another. "—who surfaced at least twice a year from that point forward, was doing their best to raise suspicions. After all, if Oren *had* been involved in Avi's death, he wouldn't have been able to benefit by it."

I sat back and crossed my arms. "Let's ignore the wack jobs for the moment. You examined him at the scene. What did you see? What do you think?"

Jerry pursed his lips, fingers laced over his belly as he squinted at the ceiling. "Avi had been in generally good spirits during the party, considering his disappointment and perhaps anger at Oren's absence. I caught the occasional expression on his face that, as a physician, told me he was experiencing discomfort, but as you know, physical and emotional discomfort can express themselves in the same ways. So other than asking him if he felt all right—which he assured me he did—I didn't press the matter." His gaze dropped to mine. "Something I've regretted to this day."

I murmured something vaguely reassuring, and Jerry smiled tightly.

"After he fell, I determined that the fall and the contusion on his forehead were not significant enough to be fatal. However, when palpating his scalp, I found a raised lump the circumference of a golf ball just above his hairline at the base of his skull. I believe he'd struck his head at some point within the previous seventy-two hours, resulting in bleeding in the brain."

"Subdural hematoma."

"Exactly. But as his advanced directive and cultural/religious customs prohibited autopsy, since it was clear doing so wouldn't provide any service to the living, I was only able to conduct non-invasive examinations. These confirmed what I'd suspected, but gave no additional information, and since there was no evidence of a crime—Avi himself had never mentioned hitting his head, although Ricky said he'd seen him taking ibuprofen for some kind of pain—there was no reason to countermand his wishes."

"Do you think it was an accident?"

"It's a possibility."

I tilted my head, lifting an eyebrow. "Do you think there are other possibilities?"

He met my gaze. "The back of his head obviously came into contact with a heavy object, applied with some force, at some point before the party. In hindsight, I sincerely doubt that level of impact could have occurred accidentally."

"Meaning?"

"Meaning"—Jerry's expression hardened—"some *asshole* bashed him on the head."

Chapter Sixteen

I frowned, rubbing the back of my head at a twinge of sympathetic pain. "Wouldn't he have, you know, *noticed* something like that?"

"Not necessarily." Jerry closed the folio. "If it knocked him out, which I judge a blow of that severity would do, he might not recall what had happened when he awoke. That kind of contextual amnesia is common with sudden traumatic events, such as car crashes, or, as I understand, childbirth." He chuckled again. "I can't tell you how many of my female patients declare during labor with their second, third, or even fourth child that if they'd remembered how much it hurt, they would have never let their husbands near them again."

"Do you think—" My cell phone beeped in my pocket and I winced. "Sorry. I should have silenced it when we came inside."

He gestured expansively. "Do you see any other patrons whom you're disturbing? Please. Go ahead and take your call." He pushed the folio across the desk to me. "Feel free to look over these articles afterward. I have some puttering to do for our next book club meeting."

He left the Reference desk and disappeared into the stacks as I wrestled my phone out of my pocket. The number was unfamiliar.

"Hello?" I said, keeping my voice low because even though nobody else was here, it was still a freaking *library*.

"Is this Maz Armani?"

"Maz *Amani*. Yes."

"Oh. Right." The man on the line chortled. "I made that mistake before, didn't I?"

"Carson?"

"You remembered! Yes, Carson Clemenson. I just wanted to see how you were settling in and if you were ready to escape to someplace a little more civilized yet."

I frowned. "I'm not exactly in the middle of the Gobi desert."

"No, no. Of course not. It's only that Ghost has, shall we say, limited entertainment choices? I promised you a coffee date. Would now be convenient?"

"Now?" Jeez, nothing like giving a guy some advance notice.

"Just coffee. It's the middle of the morning, so a good time for a break, don't you think? There's a Starbucks in Richdale, if you'd like to meet me there in twenty minutes or so."

I was about to refuse, but then I realized Carson, as Avi's cousin, might have insight into his life and relationships that mere friends like Saul and Jerry, or casual workers like Ricky, wouldn't have. I couldn't tell you why I was suddenly so obsessed with Avi's death—okay, yes, I could, and it was the fact that Avi was still living in my house even though he was, well, *not* living in my house—but I was determined to find out everything I could about him. If I understood him better, even if I couldn't get him to, I don't know, move toward the light or whatever, I could at least negotiate a peaceful cohabitation.

"Actually, Carson, I'd love to meet up, but I've started a new job today and I don't have the time to drive into Richdale. What about Isaksen's here in Ghost?" I'd noticed as I'd passed last night that they had a dozen or so small tables inside. "Do they serve coffee?"

"Yeeesss," Carson drawled. "But *Starbucks*—"

"If you could meet me at Isaksen's in twenty minutes, I'll have about half an hour to spare."

I could hear his huff of exasperation over the phone. "All right. But only for you." His voice held a flirty edge. "It's not every day an attractive new man comes to town."

Don't pour it on too thick, Carson. I'd seen his clothes. His shoes. His car. And he'd seen mine. We were definitely not on the same style or wealth wavelength. But then I gave myself a mental bitch-slap for making assumptions based on appearances. Maybe Carson was interested in the *inner* me. Maybe he saw *beyond* downscale vehicles and low-end fashion choices. I needed to give him a chance, because even if I didn't want to date him, I really wanted to pick his brain.

Not allowing him an opportunity to change his mind, I blurted, "Thanks! I'll see you then!" in far too hearty a tone, and disconnected the call.

I spent the next fifteen minutes reading over the articles in the scrapbook. To tell the truth, they kind of broke my heart. The reporter had interviewed Avi before the party, and he'd been so upbeat and cheerful, excited to show everyone what he and Oren had accomplished, thrilled that Oren was ready to make Ghost his permanent home. He'd interviewed other people too —the couple who owned the B & B that Oren had helped renovate, the brother and sister who ran the bakery. Not Carson, I noted, although he was quoted in the article following Avi's death.

I checked the time. *Oops.* I needed to meet Carson like now, so I snapped pictures of all the articles with my phone—no flash, of course—and closed the folio carefully. I found Jerry in the fiction section, in front of the *Fa - Fi* shelf. He was thumbing through *Behind Time,* Jake Fields' third book, and, in my opinion, his best.

"Hey, Jerry. Thanks so much for opening up for me and sharing all the information about Avi."

He smiled warmly at me. "My pleasure."

I flicked a finger at the book. "Book club making its way through Jake's work?"

"What?" He chuckled and shelved the book. "No. Just nostalgic, I guess."

"Yeah. His last book wasn't really up to his usual standard, was it? Hope the next one's better."

His eyebrows shot up. "His next—"

"Sorry, I've got to run. Thanks again, and I'll definitely be coming by during regular hours." I grinned and ran my finger along a row of book spines. "I love the company."

I hurried out the door and down the street. Luckily, Isaksen's was only half a block away, so I was still a couple of minutes early. I didn't see Carson's shiny car at the curb, and when I walked into the bakery to the cheerful accompaniment of tinkling bells, I didn't spot him inside either.

Instead, Taryn stood at the register, leaning over the counter as she smiled up at a tall, red-haired woman in a sleeveless T-shirt that exposed some serious arm definition, her pale skin liberally sprinkled with freckles. An Asian man with his long black hair caught up in a ponytail backed through a swinging door, a tray of glistening miniature fruit tarts in his hands.

His smile was nearly as bright as the lights in the display case where he deftly unloaded the pastries. "Welcome to Isaksen's. You must be Maz."

I blinked. "Um, yes?"

Taryn looked over at me and burst out laughing. "The look on your face. Don't worry. I told them both about you. Jae-Seong isn't psychic."

He gave her a glare of mock outrage. "How dare you! I'll have you know I aced my History of Tarot test precisely because I could read Professor DeHaven's mind."

"Yeah," drawled the red-haired woman. "Couldn't be because you stayed up half the night studying before the final."

He sighed dramatically. "Nobody appreciates my talents."

"*I* appreciate them," Taryn said. "And Maz will too when you make him one of your signature Vietnamese coffees." She turned to face me. "Maz, these two goofballs are Haley and Jae-Seong Isaksen. They own the bakery."

"Took over from our parents," Haley said. "Who are now off traveling and enjoying their retirement."

"And we," Jae-Seong said, "enjoy them not looking over our shoulder and micromanaging everything from the decor to the sourdough starter."

Taryn patted her ample hip. "I owe much of my padding to their work, especially since they never charge me for anything and it's hard to resist a poppyseed scone or giant cinnamon roll when it's free."

"We owe your pop more than free baked goods for life," Jae-Seong said. "If it weren't for him, our folks would never have found us and made us a family."

Taryn grinned. "He is good, isn't he?" She smiled at Haley. "Will I see you for dinner tonight?"

"Definitely." Haley leaned over the counter and planted a kiss on Taryn's lips, lingering just long enough that their relationship was not in the least in question. "Jae-Seong's doing the bread prep tonight, so I'm free."

"Excellent." Taryn pointed at Jae-Seong. "Remember. Vietnamese coffee for Maz." She lifted her nose in the air. "You can put it on my tab."

Jae-Seong laughed and tossed a blue and white striped napkin at her, which she snatched out of the air. "Get out of here, woman. You're distracting my sister."

She laughed and faced me. "Maz, I'm glad I ran into you. The delivery company will be dropping off Oren's effects tomorrow sometime between eight and noon. Will that be convenient?"

I screwed up my face. "I'm not sure? I've just started at the Manor and I already bugged out on your dad this morning to check on something in the library."

"Don't worry. He'll understand." She dug her phone out of her purse. "How about this? I'll have them text you when they're ten minutes out. If you're just at the Manor, you can be there to meet them, no problem." She winked. "Dad's not as much of a cruel task master as he looks."

"Are you kidding? He's like a cross between a tall, shaped-up Santa and everybody's favorite uncle. I find it hard to believe he's ever said a cross word in his life."

She chuckled and patted my arm. "Trust me. He uttered plenty of cross words when I was a teenager. Dad and Pop both did, because I dearly loved to test boundaries. Still do, in fact." She fluttered her fingers at Jae-Seong, blew a kiss at Haley and headed for the door just as Carson stepped inside. "Morning, Carson. Slumming?"

He gave her a tight-lipped smile. "Always a pleasure, Taryn." He held the door for her, giving her a little bow as she sailed past.

Chapter Seventeen

Carson shut the door behind Taryn and then turned to me with a smile while dusting off his palms. "Sorry if I'm late. My client meeting ran a bit long."

"No worries. I just got here myself. Haven't even had time to pick out a pastry."

His glance flicked up and down my body. "Well, *you* at least have room for a treat now and then. There's a wonderful boulangerie in Richdale that does a hazelnut cream religieuse to die for. I'll bring you one."

Since Carson A) made a body-shaming remark that I was glad Taryn wasn't present to hear and B) disparaged the bakery's wares, I glanced at the Isaksens, hoping they hadn't overheard. Judging by Haley's frown and Jae-Seong's eye-roll, though, that hope was obviously forlorn.

"Thanks, but I'm sure I'll find something perfect here. Ricky brought me the pumpkin spice muffin this morning and it was awesome." I pointed at the quesitos, their pastry envelopes perfectly browned, the cheese filling peeking out from under the guava paste. "I've had my eye on those since I walked in. In fact, could I have two, please? No, make that three."

"Fantastic choice," Haley said. She faced Carson with the air of someone girding for battle. "What can I get for you, Carson?"

"I'll have a nonfat flat white with Tenesor's single origin Kaffa. Continental roast, of course."

"We don't have that."

"No? In Richdale, I can get it—"

"We've got Cusmaan Kaffa. It's from the same region, but it's fair trade." Haley bared her teeth in a feral smile. "Continental roast, of course."

"Hmmm. I suppose that will have to do." Carson handed over his Amex Black without looking at her.

By that point, if I didn't need Carson's insights on Avi, I would have bailed. Because being rude to service workers? Nope.

After Haley rang up his order, she slapped his card down on the counter. "Always a pleasure, Carson."

I wasn't certain if she was purposely echoing his remark to Taryn, but it seemed a bit too pointed not to be intentional.

Carson must have read my expression, because he chuckled as he slipped the card back in his wallet. "You'll have to excuse our little banter. We've known each other most of our lives."

"Yeah," Jae-Seong said over the hiss of the espresso machine. "We've got *history*."

I wondered briefly what that *history* entailed. Had Carson and Jae-Seong dated? Carson and Haley? Carson and *Taryn*? None of those matches seemed likely, but my poor track record with men was legendary, so it's not like I was a reliable authority. Besides, it wasn't any of my business.

I reached for my own wallet. "What do I owe you?"

Haley held up her palm. "You're on Taryn's tab, remember?"

I squirmed a little, wondering if Taryn had mentioned my financially challenged state, but hey, I'd jettisoned my pride the first time I'd surfed a couch, so I just said, "Thank you," and meant it. Big time.

Behind me, Carson chuckled. "Don't worry. I'm sure Taryn will bill you for it later. She never gives anything away for free, not even to friends."

My gaze bounced between the three of them. "Uh…"

"It's coffee and a few pastries, Carson," Haley said, "not hours of legal services, which, by the way, would have been a conflict of interest for her. Besides, I don't recall you waiving your commission when she bought her house."

Carson sighed. "Be reasonable, Haley. It was my first sale."

"Exactly," she said.

"My hands were tied. My broker wouldn't allow it."

"Whatever." She turned to me and smiled. "Please ignore our"—her gaze slid sidelong to Carson—"*banter*, Maz. Welcome to Ghost. Have a seat and we'll bring everything to you when the coffee's ready."

"Great. Um, thanks."

"So, Maz." Carson motioned for me to follow him to a table in the corner. "How are you settling in? I know the first days after a move can be disorienting. New places, new people, new experiences."

"You can say that again," I muttered.

He'd angled his chair so his back was to the counter and catercorner from the other chair, which was backed against the window. Unless I wanted to make a big production out of moving mine, I'd be sitting almost knee to knee with him. I settled for scooting my chair a little farther away under the guise of moving it closer to the table as I sat.

"I always tell my clients the best way to acclimate to your new surroundings is to invite friends over right away. Forge positive connections. Lay the foundation for your network immediately."

"Really?" I asked, a little dubious. *My* first inclination had been to revel in the new space alone with Gil. Even if I hadn't ended up towing Ricky along with me, that wouldn't been an option, anyway, since the house had come with a preexisting roommate.

And when I say *preexisting,* I mean that in *all* senses of the word.

"Absolutely. It's been proven by tons of studies." He tapped his temple with his forefinger. "It's all about brain science."

I'd vetted more books than I cared to remember where the "studies" had been based on poor data quality or statistically insignificant sample sets, so I just shrugged. "No friends to invite over quite yet."

"Oh, that won't do! If you want, I can toddle on over tonight with some lovely takeout from this Oaxacan place in Richdale. Very elevated. You'll love it."

I chuckled a little uneasily. "I'm not sure I'm an elevated kind of guy. Besides, we've got a terrific Mexican place practically next door."

"Yes, but—"

"Flat white." Jae-Seong arrived with a tray and plonked a heavy ceramic mug in front of Carson. "And for you, Maz, the quesitos." He slid a blue-patterned plate onto the table, the pastries arranged in a fan, and presented my cup—clear glass rather than ceramic—like it was an Oscar statuette. The liquid was layered—golden on the bottom, rich dark brown on the top. "And a Vietnamese coffee, as instructed." He handed me a small silver spoon. "Give it a stir before you taste."

Since he waited expectantly, the empty tray held in front of him, I swirled the spoon, combining the layers, and then took a sip. My eyes widened. "Wow!" I took a bigger gulp, not caring if the heat singed my tongue a little because it was worth it for the *flavor*. Rich, dark, sweet, with a hint of hazelnut. "This is *fantastic*."

He grinned at me. "Glad you like it. I'll make it for you anytime."

I shot him a thumbs-up, and he sauntered back to where Haley was leaning over the counter, watching us with a smirk.

When I returned my attention to Carson, he was looking a little sulky. I supposed I couldn't blame him. He'd invited me out, but I'd essentially commandeered the meet-up by insisting we come here, where there were apparently long-standing *undercurrents* that I couldn't hope to parse immediately. Nor was I sure I wanted to. I was the new guy. I couldn't hope to understand the nuances of relationships that had been built over lifetimes. Maybe I should approach Ghost and its denizens like I would any project: Collect as much information as I could without drawing early conclusions that could jeopardize my objectivity.

I offered Carson a smile over the rim of my cup. "Thanks for agreeing to meet me here. Since I'm just starting work at the Manor, I didn't really want to take too much time away on my first day."

He studied me, his head tilted to one side and a faint smile on his lips. With the sun through the window glinting on his golden hair, I could admit he was a very attractive man. For that matter, so was Jae-Seong, who'd given me more than one flirty glance. How likely was it that I'd land in a teensy town like Ghost and run into not one, not two, but three men who might be interested in me?

Jeez, Maz, objectivity. Ob-jec-tivity. Chances were much greater that people were just being friendly. In a small town, anybody new was bound to rouse interest, and that interest didn't have to be romantic.

"Are you sure you're all right?" Carson asked gently. "If you don't mind my saying so, you're looking a little uncomfortable. There's still time to go to Richdale. Or even back to your place, if that works better for you."

"No, no. I'm fine here." I took another sip of the fabulous coffee and tried not to moan. "And I'm starting to get used to my house." And its attendant ghost. More or less.

He gave me a wide smile. "There's a lot to get used to, isn't there? It's the third largest house in town, after the Manor and the old Jenkins place."

The name pinged a memory from the morning. "I think Saul mentioned that house. It's a B & B now, isn't it?"

He wrinkled his slightly snub nose. "Struggling, but yes."

"You, um, probably spent a lot of time in my house back in the day." I winced internally. Not exactly a smooth segue.

"I did. Not as much as Ricky and Liam, perhaps, since Sofia was right next door and my parents moved us to Richdale when I was in junior high."

"But you still went to school with them all? Avi, too?"

"Avi was ten years older, but the rest of us, yes. Ghost only had a K-4 elementary then, and it closed in the late nineties, anyway. We were all bused to Richdale to school after that. That's why my parents decided to move. They didn't like me being on the bus for so long every day."

"But you still spent time at the house? With Avi and his parents?"

He took a sip of his coffee, not meeting my eyes. "I did, yes." He glanced over his shoulder. "There's something you should know about Avi. Something that nobody but his closest family knew, not even Oren."

I leaned forward. This was it. What I wanted to know. The scoop. "What?"

"Avi had a dark side." He looked down at his cup. "A *very* dark side. A cruelty he was very careful not to let anybody see."

He hunched his shoulders as though expecting a blow, and a kernel of outrage burned in my middle. Ever I'd vetted a book about domestic violence for a clinical social worker, any hint of physical abuse was a trigger for me.

"Did he *hurt* you?" I hissed. "*Hit* you?"

Carson's breath hitched. "There are ways to hurt that don't involve physical violence, you know."

Boy, did I ever. Greg was a master at the sly put down, which was another reason the social worker's book had left such an enduring mark on me. "Verbal, you mean? Emotional?"

He jerked a nod. "He never missed an opportunity to cut me down, undermine my confidence, belittle my dreams. But only when nobody else was around, so there were never any witnesses to take my side." He lifted his chin, blinking rapidly as though to fight back tears, smile trembling. "But I rose above it in the end. Made a success of myself, even though I had to abandon my youthful hopes and dreams along the way."

I gripped his forearm. "It's never too late to late to follow a dream. And adult perspective might grant you new insight into those youthful hopes. You never know."

His smile grew a little wider. "Thank you, Maz. That's very kind of you. And it helps. It helps a lot." He dropped his gaze and peeked up at me through his lashes in nearly the same way as Ricky had, although it didn't hit me low in the belly the same way. "Maybe we could get together again sometime? I'd love to come over and cook for you."

I blinked. "You cook?"

He chuckled. "Well, I can dish up takeout with the best of them. What do you say?"

"I'll keep that in mind once I'm a little more settled in."

He clucked his tongue and shook his head. "Remember what I said. The best way to settle in is to invite friends over."

"Maybe. But I'm not quite at that point yet. Still a lot of loose ends to tie up." Like whether the resident ghost would reveal his dark side in the middle of a dinner party. "But I've got your number, so I'll be sure to let you know when I'm ready."

His lips thinned for an instant, but then they relaxed. If he'd been abused or belittled in the past, I imagine he might take my words as a rejection. But I really couldn't risk having anyone else over. Not now that I knew a little more about Avi and his death.

I wondered what Marguerite Windflower charged for her video exorcism service. Because regardless of my initial compassion for Avi and Oren and their doomed love story, I wasn't about to let a possibly abusive ghost drive me out of *my house.*

Chapter Eighteen

I spent the rest of the day sorting through the contents of the Manor's document room. It was more organized than I'd had any right to hope, and I was actually getting excited about the project. Then, at four, my phone rang.

Oh shit. Ricky.

"Heeey, I'm glad you called."

"Uh oh," he replied, a smile in his tone. "Sounds like you're about to bail on our dinner date."

I stood up, pressing a hand to my back where my two nights on the floor and six hours of shuffling crates around were making themselves felt. "A rain check? I'm more beat than I thought I'd be. Guess I've been spending too much time sitting at my laptop and not enough time at the gym. I need to start working out more if I'm going to be deadlifting crates full of papers and books."

"I understand. Don't feel obligated."

"It's not that!" I said hurriedly. "I really do want to go out with you. Get to know you. Get to know more about Ghost. But I'd be lousy company tonight." Especially if I had yet another night on the floor to look forward to.

"Hey, man, like I said. We're cool. Can I give you a call in a day or two, after you've had a chance to get used to your new normal?"

"I'd like that." And I liked that he didn't push. "Thanks."

"*De nada*. Talk soon."

I sighed as I disconnected the call. I couldn't deny that I was a little let down. I'd been looking forward to seeing Ricky again, but yawning in his face for the entire date was not the way to make an impression.

At just after five, I locked up the document room with the key Saul had given me for the duration of the project. "Considering the scope of what you'll be working with," he'd said with a chuckle, "you might be carrying it for the rest of your life."

I could think of worse fates. Steady work, friendly client, interesting project, and the freedom to shape it the way I'd like? Yeah, I'd take it and run with it as long as I could. Plus, it meant I could turn down that dreadful project that had earned Avi's disdain.

I stuck my head in Saul's office. "Goodnight. I'll be back in the morning, bright and early."

"Excellent." He pushed his keyboard aside. "And Maz? If Avi should manifest again?"

"I'll call you and Professor DeHaven. I promise."

His smile was blinding. Yeah, Jerry was on to a good thing with his husband—although after meeting the doctor-turned-librarian, I was certain the reverse was also true. "Thank you. See you tomorrow."

I whistled as I left the building and climbed into the Civic. I winced and slapped the steering wheel. "Ah, crap."

I'd intended to ask Saul whether it was okay for me to walk across the grounds—it was practically a straight shot from my house to the Manor, albeit through some pretty dense woods. However, I wasn't sure if that was allowed or if there was even a break in the fence that would let me enter without coming all the way around to the main gates, anyway. Even so, a nice brisk walk—as long as it wasn't raining—would be a good way to start my new fitness regime.

"Cardio to go with the weights," I muttered as I turned onto Main Street. "That's a plan."

Since I had to collect Gil from Sofia, I used the fob to open the garage and pull inside, but didn't enter the house yet. Instead, I used the keypad to close the door and crossed the front lawn, gazing up through the unfurling maple leaves at the sky. I sniffed the air appreciatively. Clean and spring crisp, scented with damp earth and mown grass rather than car exhaust. Yeah, I could get used to small town living, if this was what it was like.

I mounted Sofia's porch steps and knocked on her door. I heard footsteps approaching, but it wasn't Sofia who opened the door.

"Ricky?" I said, a smile splitting my face. "What are you doing here?"

He shrugged, meeting my goofy smile with one of his own. "Tia needed some new blinds hung in the spare room." He pushed open the screen door. "Come on in. Although I'll warn you—you might not be able to pry her away from Gil. She's fallen hard for him. Even made him her special cat treats."

"In that case, I might not be able to pry *him* away from *her*. The way to Gil's heart is directly through his belly." I walked inside and was immediately overcome by a heavenly aroma. "If that's what her cat treats smell like, I might just wrestle Gil for them. Although he'd probably win."

Ricky chuckled and gestured for me to follow him through a scrupulously clean living room smelling faintly of citrus and populated with overstuffed furniture in bright colors. "That's her pozole. She baked the gatito galletas earlier."

We entered the kitchen, a big, farmhouse-style room, its walls painted a cheery red with sunny yellow accents, hand-painted tiles featuring roosters and chickens marching along the backsplash. Gil was perched on a barstool, his head clearing the counter as he watched Sofia slice an avocado.

"Maz!" she cried. "You are just in time for dinner."

"It smells amazing, Sofia, but I couldn't impose."

"Pffft." She flapped her hands at me. "It is no imposition. Especially if you set the table and help Enrique wash up afterward."

Ricky leaned over and stage whispered from behind his hand. "Resistance is futile."

Sofia shook a finger at him. "Don't be fresh, Enrique. Show Maz where the plates are and then pour the iced tea."

"Yes, Tia," he said humbly, but gave me a wink when he kissed her cheek.

Ricky pointed at a glass-fronted cupboard full of mugs and plates that matched the kitchen's vibrant colors. I reached for them, but hesitated. "May I wash up first?"

"What a considerate boy. Of course." She nodded toward the living room. "Enrique will show you where."

He smiled wryly and led me back the way we'd come, to a powder room down the hall from the entry. He grimaced as he indicated the door. "Sorry. I know you wanted to go home tonight."

"I just didn't want to risk going to a restaurant when the chances were high I'd fall asleep in my plate. This is different. Trust me. I couldn't be happier."

His expression cleared. "Good. I'm glad."

"Besides…" I winked as I pushed the door open. "I don't want to offend my cat-sitter by refusing her hospitality. She might turn me down next time I need a Gil-watcher."

He barked a laugh. "Not a chance," he tossed over his shoulder as he walked back toward the kitchen. "She'll be inviting him over without you before you know it."

I washed up quickly and returned. "Just the three of us for dinner?" I asked as I opened the cabinet.

I caught an odd expression on Ricky's face as Sofia turned to me. "Set the table for four, if you please. The big bowls." She gave me a contented smile. "I always set a place for Guillermo, in case he should drop by."

At Ricky's subtle headshake, I forbore from blurting, *But I thought he was at Harvard,* and set four deep bowls on the crimson tablecloth. As we sat down, I noted that Gil had hopped onto the floor, where two matching dishes—one with water and one with what looked like minced chicken livers—were arrayed on a red and white gingham placemat. Yeah, clearly Gil was not suffering under Sofia's care. I'd be lucky to lure him back home.

Sofia held out her hands to Ricky and me. Following his example, I took hers in one hand and Ricky's in the other. "I must ask, Maz, although I mean no disrespect or intrusion. Are you of the Islam faith?"

"Er, no. My father's family was Eastern Orthodox, but I'm kind of ath—" I caught that tiny shake of Ricky's head again. "—aaagnostic."

Her brow wrinkled. "Believing in something is important for the heart as well as the head. What do you believe in?"

Yeesh. I couldn't very well say my personal altars were dedicated to the worship of grammar and narrative logic. "The Force. Between all living things."

Although Ricky rolled his eyes, Sofia nodded as though satisfied. "Yes, we are all linked, but you must not limit yourself to the living."

I thought about Avi lurking somewhere in my house. "I'm starting to see that."

"We are Catholic here," she said, although Ricky mouthed *lapsed,* morphing his silent word into a smile when Sofia shot a sharp glance his way, "so I always begin a meal with grace. Although, since Guillermo said it sometimes makes others uncomfortable, I always say my prayer silently."

I was starting to get really ticked off at Guillermo or Liam or whatever he called himself. Personally, I'd call him a jerk. "I don't mind. If you want to speak aloud, go ahead."

She squeezed my hand, smiling even as she shook her head. Then she closed her eyes and her lips began moving silently. I was pretty good at lip-reading after working with several clients who were hearing-impaired, but I didn't recognize anything Sofia was saying. I suspected she was speaking in Spanish, with which I only had enough experience to read menus and ask *dónde está el baño?* But with a sidelong glance at Ricky, I suspected that DuoLingo was in my future.

Sofia opened her eyes again and released our hands. "Now eat, eat. Boys are always hungry, I know. Enrique, would you serve us, please? Our guest first."

I passed my bowl to Ricky, and he ladled it full of the fragrant pozole. "I'm almost thirty, Tia. And I suspect Maz is about the same age."

I nodded. "Thirty last February."

"See? We're hardly boys anymore."

"Pffft. You are all boys to me."

I took a bite and the complex flavors bloomed across my tongue—chiles and oregano and cumin and the richness of pork. "Wow, Sofia, this is amazing. I thought the cochinita pibil at Taqueria Vargas was the best thing I'd ever had, but this is better."

She chuckled as she garnished her stew with an avocado slice. "That's because Maria never adds the ghost peppers. She's afraid it will make things too hot for the customers, but I say a little bit enhances the flavors."

I paused, my spoon halfway to my open mouth, and Ricky laughed at my obvious confusion. "Tia Sofia and my abuelo started Taqueria Vargas. They still use her recipes, except when my mother makes changes." She harrumphed, and he patted her hand. "Don't worry, Tia. When Felicia takes over, she'll put the ghost peppers back in."

She nodded decisively. "She is a good girl, your sister. Her tres leches cake might be better than mine someday."

I perked up at that. "They have tres leches cake? It's one of my favorites, but I didn't see it on the menu."

"Only for special days," Sofia said. She patted my hand again. "And having a new neighbor, a new friend, is the most special of days. That is why I made one today. Finish your pozole. We will enjoy a slice together, and then I will give you some to take home."

Chapter Nineteen

"Oh, man." I rubbed my stomach, my jeans feeling decidedly tight around my middle. "That was a fantastic meal. Thank your aunt again for me."

Ricky laughed as we meandered across Sofia's front yard toward my house, him with a plate holding half the tres leches cake and me with Gil in his carrier and a bag of Sofia's homemade cat treats in my pocket

"You thanked her yourself. More times than I can count."

"Well, one more wouldn't hurt. Especially since she's watching Gil for me again tomorrow." I glanced at him sidelong. "So. I've gotta ask."

"Yeah?" Ricky raised his eyebrows as he drew out the word.

"What's the deal with Guillermo? Liam? Whatever the heck his name is?"

This time, Ricky's laugh held an edge of relief, and I wondered for a moment what he was afraid I was going to ask. "The guy's a total tool. That's the deal. But Tia thinks he walks on water, which might be the only thing the two of them have in common."

"Wow, Ricky," I said, deadpan. "Harsh."

"True, though." He sighed. "I'd like to say he was better when he was a kid, but not really. Only child of Tia's only son, who married the boss's daughter when he was working his way up the corporate ladder."

I blinked at him. "Ghost has a corporation big enough to have a ladder?"

"The corporation—or at least its branch—was in Richdale."

"Was?"

"Yeah, it closed down when we were in high school, right about the time Tio Lorenzo Type-A'd himself into an early heart attack."

I winced. "I'm sorry."

Ricky managed to wave my words away while keeping the cake perfectly balanced. "It was a while ago, and we didn't see him much after he took over the business from his father-in-law. Although to give him credit, he used to make sure Liam stayed with Tia Sofia every summer for at least a month, so we got to know him even before we all got shipped to Richdale for school." He smiled a little crookedly. "He pretty much ignored us even then, holed up in his room and playing video games, except when Tia gave him the choice of working in her garden with her or hanging out with us. He never had much use for any of us even then, except maybe for Carson eventually."

"Ah. That was something else I wanted to ask you about." I slowed to a stop halfway across my lawn. "I met Carson for coffee at Isaksen's today."

Ricky grimaced. "Ouch."

"Yeah, I kinda got that there might be some drama there."

"You could say so. Carson and Jae-Seong were sort of going out in high school—or at least approaching the tipping point—but it fizzled once Carson and Liam formed their Young Assholes of America bond." He sighed again. "Although it would have fizzled, anyway. The rest of us could see the writing on the wall, but Haley made the mistake of telling Jae-Seong that, which made him dig in his heels and hold on a lot longer than I think even he wanted. It, ah, got a little messy."

I thought back to what Carson had told me about Avi. Since Ricky seemed to be in a mood to share, I decided to push a little more.

"Do you think Carson's behavior might have been the result of... other pressures? Issues of self-confidence, maybe? Or safety?"

Ricky turned to face me fully, eyes narrowing. "Let me guess. He told you that Avi was mean to him, right?"

The handle of Gil's carrier was cutting into my palm because I was gripping it so hard, so I set it on the grass. "Actually, he implied it was beyond just being mean. More like emotional abuse."

He shook his head. "Impossible. Look, his mom and Carson's were sisters. Close. Spent a lot of time together. But Avi was a decade older than us and an introvert to boot, so when the families got together, Carson would have been by himself if he wasn't hanging out with me, Haley, Taryn, and Jae-Seong. Think about it. There's a huge difference between six and sixteen or even thirteen and twenty-three. Those divides don't start leveling out until everyone's at least a technical adult."

"That's fair, I guess." I picked up Gil's carrier again, and we ambled to the porch, mounting the steps slowly. "Is there some reason Carson would blame Avi for destroying his dreams?"

"Dreams? Carson?" Ricky barked a laugh as he set the cake on the porch railing. I nearly lunged for it, but he stopped me with a touch on my chest. "Don't worry. The rail cap is wide. The plate won't fall."

"Sorry. It's just really good cake."

"It is." He nodded toward the porch swing. "I won't ask to come in, since I know you're tired. But will you sit for a moment? I think we should finish this conversation."

"Okay," I croaked, wondering where my breath had disappeared to. I set Gil's carrier on the porch, but misjudged the distance to the ground for some reason. He protested the resulting thump with a yowl. "Sorry, boy." I settled onto the swing next to Ricky.

It wasn't that wide.

My hip brushed his, our knees knocked together, his shoulder was warm against mine. He didn't apologize. Neither did I. I studied his profile as he gnawed on his lower lip, gazing into the dark.

Finally, he shot me an apologetic smile. "Didn't mean to get all pensive. I was just wondering how to put this. Everyone has their own…" He gestured, his hands sketching a circle in the air. "I don't know… world view? Carson's pretty firmly at the center of his."

"Aren't we all? At least to some extent?"

He shrugged. "I suppose. And Carson isn't quite as self-centered as Liam. But he grants more importance to tangible objects and possessions, maybe because his dad had a tendency to make regular sweeps of their house and donate everything he didn't think was necessary anymore. He… latches on to things. Assigns them relative value. And naturally assigns his own interests more value than anyone else's."

"Is that why he expected Taryn to provide legal services for free?"

He chuckled. "That came up at the bakery, huh? I'm not surprised. If Haley and Carson are in the same space for more than ten minutes, it's bound to."

"Taryn was there at first, too."

"Ooh. Double whammy."

I frowned, tilting my head. "Interestingly enough, he didn't expect to get his coffee for free."

Ricky widened his eyes and gave me a faux-shock expression. "But that's *coffee*."

"So coffee has more value than legal services?"

"In Carson's mind, yes. Because coffee is a physical thing, composed of other physical things. Commodities like beans and water and cups that cost the bakery to deliver. In his mind, it's a fair trade to pay for that. But Taryn's legal advice doesn't cost her anything to provide."

"Other than her time and expertise," I said dryly.

He waggled a finger. "Time and expertise have no inventory. Besides, haven't you heard? Talk is cheap."

"Depends on who's talking. There are some people I'd pay *not* to listen to." I leaned back, the swing's slats cradling my spine. "But as somebody who makes his living with words, I take exception to them not having the same value as bacon or orange juice or… or coffee just because you can't hold them in your hands. Besides, isn't Carson a real estate agent? He *literally* gets paid for his time."

"I don't think that's how he sees it. He's getting paid for the *house*, which you have to admit is pretty dang physical."

"I suppose."

"Maz." Ricky's voice was a little hoarse when he said my name, which did interesting things to my insides. He cleared his throat. "I know you don't know me well. You don't really know anyone in town yet, although you probably know more about them now."

I winced. "Sorry. Was I being nosy? Occupational hazard. I'm hard-wired for research."

"Not a problem." His face was so close. I could see the gleam in his dark eyes by the glow of the porch light. "But since I've answered your questions, could you tell me one thing?"

"S-sure." *So close.* Was he going to ask if he could kiss me? Should I ask if I could kiss *him*? We were both thirty-year-old gay men. Approximately. Surely this shouldn't be so awkward. But consent was a thing. "Ask away."

"Why are you afraid to leave your cat alone in your house?"

Chapter Twenty

I jerked back. "What?"

He glanced down at Gil, who had folded his front paws under him, his eyes slitted nearly closed, probably in a chicken-liver coma. "He doesn't seem skittish. Quite the opposite. Are you afraid he'll damage something in the house?

"No. No, that's not it."

"Then what?" He placed a gentle hand on my knee. "I'd say to trust me, but trust is something that's built over time, not something that's granted by default. But I'd like to be your friend." His lips quirked. "Maybe more, if things work out. So if there's anything you want to share, anything that I can help with, I'm here."

Could I tell him about Avi? He hadn't been able to see him, although he'd seen the results of the library tornado. But it was one thing to see physical evidence of something—something I might just as easily have staged myself. It was another to blurt out *I see dead people. One dead person anyway. Oh, and incidentally? He was a friend of yours.*

I dropped my gaze to his hand on my knee. Would he think I was hallucinating? In need of medication? Of psychiatric help? Heck, did *I* think that? I was strongly attracted to Ricky and thought he was attracted to me, too. But if I expected us to act on what seemed to be a mutual feeling and take it further, I didn't want to hide things from him now that might come back and bite me on the butt later.

Building trust. Yeah, that. Might as well start now. His reaction might give me all the answers I needed.

"The thing is," I said, my voice probably a little too soft because he leaned closer. Not that I was complaining about *that*. "I'm afraid the house is haunted."

"Yes. Saul and Professor DeHaven seemed very excited about the… event. Is that why you don't want to leave Gil there alone? In case something similar happens?"

That was the truth, as far as it went. I could stop there and he'd understand. *But I'd still be hiding something. The Big Thing.* "Yes." I swallowed hard. "Because he's unpredictable."

Ricky's brows snapped together. "Gil?"

"No. I can pretty much predict what he'll do. His repertoire isn't that large. Eat. Sleep. Shed."

"Then who?"

Here goes nothing. "Avi."

He stared at me blankly. "Avi. The Avi who lived in this house? Avi Felder?" I nodded. "You saw *Avi's ghost*?"

"Actually, I saw him twice. But, um, you didn't."

The frown was back. "What do you mean?"

"Remember when you thought I was asking about the blinds?"

"That was just yesterday, so yeah."

"Avi was at the table, staring at my laptop. He, um, objects to the quality of writing on a prospective project."

Ricky's smile dawned. "Well, he was a writer. It was probably professional outrage. He hated sloppy prose."

I blinked. "Wait. You believe me? You don't think I'm… imagining things?"

Ricky bumped my shoulder with his own. "My family celebrates Dia de los Muertos. In fact, the whole town does. The town is literally called Ghost. What makes you think I'd be skeptical about a sighting?"

I was a little miffed, if I was honest with myself. I'd expected the reveal to create a bigger reaction, something more than

Ricky's unruffled acceptance. Where was the drama? The amazement? The horror?

"Well, *I'm* skeptical, so I think my apprehension is understandable. For all I knew, you'd run off and warn the whole town that I was a con man. Or else contact the authorities and have me hauled away for a mandatory 72-hour psych eval."

"Maz." He rose and looked down at me, his expression serious but somehow still open. "I promise I'm not dismissing your concerns, and if you'd still rather not trust Gil in the house alone, Tia Sofia will be happy to take care of him. But I'd like to help, if you'll let me." He held out his hand with a tentative smile. "So will you invite me inside?"

I gazed at his hand for a moment, probably a little too long because he started to withdraw it, his smile fading. So I grabbed it and stood up, nearly overbalancing him until I caught his other arm to steady him. "Okay. It's possible nothing will happen, though."

"Hey, this is Ghost." He grinned. "I'm game either way."

I fit the key in the lock, and for a wonder, it turned easily. I shot a glance over my shoulder. "At least the keyholes aren't jammed with sawdust again. My request must have worked."

He lifted one eyebrow. "Request?"

"When I left, I called out a plea not to stuff sawdust in the keyholes again. You know, just in case Avi was responsible."

"To tell you the truth, ghost interference makes more sense than super speedy mason bees."

I glared at him, my hand on the doorknob. "Are you taking the piss?" Greg certainly wouldn't have passed up the opportunity.

"No, I'm serious. Nothing natural could have filled up the locks that fast. While it might have been kids messing around, the kids in town don't come over here uninvited. Professor DeHaven freaks them out." He leaned closer and whispered, "They're sure she's a witch."

"It's a distinct possibility. Ready?" At his nod, I took a breath and opened the door—

And stumbled back into Ricky. Because Avi was standing in the middle of the vestibule, wringing his hands, his eyes wide.

"Man, good thing I wasn't holding the cake," Ricky said. "Did you trip?"

"No," I husked. "He's here. There."

"Who? Avi?" Ricky peered over my shoulder. "I don't see anything."

"He's standing just beyond the door." I brushed my hands down my shirt, my palms damp. "Avi? What's the matter?"

"Someone was here!" Even though his voice still sounded as though it were filtered by distance, I could hear the edge of panic.

"Where?"

He stamped his foot, which, I was interested to note, made zero impression on the hall runner. "In the *house*."

"I realize that," I said with some asperity. "I meant where in the house?"

"I don't know," Avi mumbled.

I propped my hands on my hips. "Well, that's just great. How do you know somebody was here? Did you feel a disturbance in the Force or something?"

He narrowed his eyes. "Don't patronize me, Maz."

"Sorry."

"Did he say somebody was in the house?" Ricky whispered.

I nodded. "Yep. Although I'm not sure where or why he thinks so."

"Stop talking about me as though I'm not here," Avi snapped.

"From Ricky's perspective, you *aren't* here. He can't see you."

Avi's brows lifted toward his hairline. "He can't?" I shook my head. "So why can you?"

I shrugged. "No idea." I glanced over my shoulder at Ricky. "He wants to know why I can see him, but you can't." I turned back to Avi before he blew a gasket. "Let's table that discussion for later. Where were you when the intruder arrived?"

His shoulders slumped. "I don't know that either. I was..."

"Grieving?" I asked gently. He had only just realized Oren was dead—and that he himself was no longer among the alive and kicking.

He nodded. "When I'm not here, in the house, I'm just... *not*."

"Not what?"

"Not anything. Not anywhere. But I could tell that somebody was moving around in the house. I felt it. Here." He thumped his chest with a fist, but it made no noise. "I didn't know what it meant at first. I thought it was just because I was sad."

"So it *was* a disturbance in the Force!" I crowed. When he glared at me, I held up my hands. "Sorry. But it's the best metaphor I can think of right now. This house is your space—that is, I assume you don't go anywhere else?"

He shook his head. "Here or nowhere."

"So if it's your space, in your present, er, incarnation, you're probably connected enough to it that you can tell something's wrong, yeah?"

"Maz," Ricky murmured, "maybe we should call Saul and Professor DeHaven."

I slapped my forehead. "Shoot! You're right. I promised them." I gave Avi a strained smile. "Is it okay if I let Saul Pasternak and Professor DeHaven know you're"—my gesture swept from his head to his feet—"manifesting?"

He bit his lip, clearly thinking. "Do you think they'll be able to see me?"

"No idea. But they investigated the library tornado—"

"Sorry about that."

"No worries. They were so excited about that, I thought they were going to plotz."

"Plotz?" A smile glimmered on Avi's transparent features, and I could suddenly see why someone like Oren, with a life and career elsewhere, would give it all up to move here and be with this man. "Aren't you Arabic, Maz? I'm the one who should be breaking out the Yiddish slang."

"Arabic *heritage*. Actually, I'm from Connecticut."

"Noted." He swept an arm out. "By all means, give them a call. I can't promise they'll see anything." Despite his grand gesture, his eyes behind his spectral glasses looked bleak and a little lost. "I haven't the vaguest idea how this works."

Chapter Twenty-One

I think Saul must have broken a land-speed record after I called him, because he showed up, panting, at the same time as Professor DeHaven, who only had to walk over from next door.

"He's here?" Saul asked between gulps of air. "Really?"

"Right there. Sitting on the second stair from the bottom." I pointed, and Avi raised a hand to wave. Saul, however, was focused at least a foot to the left of Avi's face, where Gil sat two steps up.

"Have you spoken with him this time?" Professor DeHaven asked.

"Quite a bit. He's upset because he thinks somebody was in the house while I was gone."

"Mortal or spiritus?" she asked.

I looked at Avi, who shrugged. "He doesn't know. He wasn't actually, er, manifesting at the time. Just felt that something was off."

"Well." Saul rubbed his hands together. "What do you say we inspect the house and see if we can collect any evidence, one way or the other?"

"I checked all the doors and windows," Ricky said. "It doesn't seem like anyone broke in."

"I *knew* I should have stuffed the keyholes again," Avi muttered.

"Trust me, I'm glad you didn't," I replied.

Saul gazed at me, his eyes sparkling. "He said something?"

"Yeah. He's the one who jammed the locks."

Saul practically danced with joy. "Manipulation of physical materials with a predetermined goal!"

"Uh huh." I glanced at Avi's stormy expression. "Let's get on with this, shall we?"

We started with the library. Professor DeHaven's attention immediately snapped to the shelf next to the turret. "Those books are not where I placed them. Could the intruder have moved them?"

"Yeah, um, no. Avi had a little bit of a tantrum—"

"I was *sad*!"

"—and tossed a couple of books and some papers around. I put those there."

"Ah," she said with a disapproving sniff.

We didn't find anything hinky in the library, the family room, the kitchen—in fact nothing on the first floor at all, so we all trooped to the second floor. I noted that Avi's feet sometimes seemed to meet the treads. At others, they either floated above them by an inch or so or looked as though they were embedded in the wood.

When we stepped into the main suite, Avi gasped and pointed to my suitcase, which I hadn't yet unpacked.

"Look! Someone was rifling through your belongings! Obviously looking for valuables!"

I grimaced, heat rushing up my throat because I hadn't planned on anybody viewing my less than pristine housekeeping, especially not my new employer, a guy I wanted to impress, and my neighbor who, if she could memorize the placement of all the books in the library after only a couple of hours, probably had her own house organized to within an inch of its life. It didn't help that Gil trotted over and leaped into the suitcase to make a nest amid my T-shirts.

"Nope. I, er, haven't bothered to unpack yet. That's kinda how I left it this morning. Well, without the cat."

Avi frowned at me. At first I thought he was judging me for untidiness, the way Professor DeHaven seemed to be doing. But then he reached out as though to touch me, although he stopped with a foot to spare. "Why haven't you unpacked?"

I shrugged. "I didn't want to presume. I mean, this was *your* room, yours and Oren's. I didn't want you to feel like I was taking over."

Avi's smile was wry. "Oren and I never slept in this room. *I* never slept here, because I was waiting for our first night here together. Please, Maz. It's okay for you to move in. It's your home too now."

"Uh…" That sentiment, along with Avi's gentle tone, hit me right below the heart. This was not the reaction of a selfish man —or a vengeful spirit. My concerns about his character, born from Carson's comments and diluted by Ricky's explanations, pretty much died. Maybe having an ethereal housemate wouldn't be so bad. "Thank you. But are you sure? If you want this room, I can take one of the others. It's not like there's a shortage of bedrooms."

He shook his head. "No. You take this one. I promise I'll respect your privacy and won't come in unless you invite me." He directed his gaze toward the wall, and I wondered briefly whether he could see through it to the stairs beyond. "I really prefer the attic now, to tell the truth. But it would be nice if more of my things were up there."

I turned to the others, who had been watching me, wide-eyed. "Avi says he'd like the attic to be his space now, but he'd like some of his things moved up there to make it—"

"More homey," Avi said.

"—more homey."

"I can do that," Ricky said. "Just tell me what and when. I'm used to hauling things up the stairs."

Avi smiled at him. "I always liked him. Although I think he had a bit of a crush on Oren. Not that I could blame him."

"Maybe after everyone else leaves"—Saul made a noise of protest—"you can point me to whatever you'd like. I'll tag it and Ricky will move it up when he has a chance."

Avi nodded. So did Ricky, their heads bobbing in synch, and they both said, "Sounds good to me."

"And on that note," I said, "moving on."

I fell in behind Avi and everyone else fell in behind me, but our little parade was pretty pointless. If anything had been missing—especially something small—I'd never have known. Avi just seemed bewildered, touching certain things with a spark of recognition but not searching for anything in particular.

After an hour or so of traipsing around, saying, "Anything missing?" about a billion times, Saul and Professor DeHaven left. Ricky hesitated at the door. And took my hand. My breath hitched as he smiled at me, but Avi was smirking at me from the landing, and I wasn't willing to put on a show for his benefit.

However, Ricky didn't seem to have a goodnight kiss in mind, anyway. He squeezed my hand once and let go. "Call me when it's convenient for me to move Avi's things and I'll be here."

"Thanks." I smiled down at him. "I really appreciate your support. For me and"—I jerked my head in Avi's direction—"for him."

He grinned and raised a hand in farewell to us both. "What are friends for?" As he headed down the porch steps, I scooped Gil up to keep him from following, and Avi joined me at the door.

"So we think nobody broke in?"

I shut the door. "There's no evidence of it. But you felt something and since neither one of us knows how this works, I'm not about to say you were wrong."

"I appreciate that." Avi glanced down at the floor and his see-through shoulders rose and fell once, twice, three times.

"Avi?" I reached out but hesitated before my hand met his arm. "Are you okay?"

"I don't know. Do you think it could have been another ghost?"

My skin prickled, my breath hitching. "I'm not sure, but I suppose it's possible."

"Maz." He looked up at me, his eyes wide, although I couldn't tell if the expression on his face was fear or hope. "What if… what if it was Oren?"

Chapter Twenty-Two

My knees were feeling decidedly wobbly, so I cuddled Gil to my chest for comfort until he squawked in protest and wriggled to escape.

Another ghost? I was just coming to terms with having *one*. And while this one was pretty non-threatening—sort of the Casper of Ghost, if Casper were adult, gay, and snarky—who knew what others might be like? Would I be able to see them too? If they were hostile, would I be able to protect myself? Protect Gil? Protect the house?

Protect Avi?

Because even though it had barely been twenty-four hours, and despite Carson's subtle trash talking, I felt closer to Avi than I'd ever felt to Greg. Maybe it was because of our connection to Oren, and through Oren, to the house. Since Avi couldn't figure it out any more than I could, I was a little leery of encountering any other… what did Professor DeHaven call them? Oh. *Spiritus* entities.

Regardless of what they were called, I needed fortification for this conversation, so I staggered down the hall to the kitchen. After I made a cup of tea and carved a huge piece of the tres leches cake, I settled at the table and motioned to the chair across from me with my fork.

"Please. Sit." When he didn't move, I set the fork next to the plate. "That is, *can* you sit?" Avi's glare was one of complete betrayal. "Come on, we're both still figuring this out, right? I watched you walk upstairs, but I'm not sure the stairs were necessary, since half the time you were an inch above them and the other half you were inside them. Is it just residual muscle memory? I mean, you can interact with the typewriter. And the books, given that you ripped all the pages out of one and threw the rest all over the room."

He stalked over—feet mostly on the floor—and sat down. That is, he folded his body in the shape of the chair, but his trajectory took him through the edge of the table. "That wasn't intentional. The library. I was just—" His shoulders lifted in what was clearly a sigh, although I couldn't hear him expel his breath. "Somebody who wasn't Oren was in my house. I'd been keeping it ready for him, everything perfect, because I wanted him to see it at its best."

I paused with my tea halfway to my mouth. "Wait. *You're* the reason the house was so clean when I got here?"

His brows knotted. "Of course."

"What did you do with all the dust?" I had a momentary vision of spectral Lemon Pledge.

"I—" An expression of confusion flickered over his face. "I have no idea. I just didn't want it to look like I couldn't take care of the place, if that makes sense."

Okay. So supernatural dust collection was a thing. Good to know. I took a bite of cake, and Avi's gaze tracked my fork. "Is that Sofia's tres leches cake?"

"Mmmhmmm," I mumbled around my mouthful. I swallowed and said, "Do you want some? I mean, can you eat? Drink?"

He extended his hand toward the frosting, lifting his brows. "May I?"

I pushed the plate toward him. "Knock yourself out."

He swiped a fingertip through the frosting—and I mean *through,* because the frosting remained pristine, as did his finger. "I guess not?"

I set the cake aside, because eating in front of him, now that I knew he couldn't share, seemed rude. "So the books were unintentional, an emotional reaction. But what about the typing? That seems a little more deliberate. Do you actually press the keys?"

He knotted his fingers together on the tabletop. "I don't remember." The napkins in the brass holder started to flutter, apparently the harbinger of another emotional tsunami—or at least a little squall.

"Hey." I held up my hands. "Don't worry about it. Maybe we can test it out later. Would that be okay?"

His smile was tentative, but the napkins stopped trying to stage an escape. "I'd like that."

"So." I curled my hands around my teacup. "Can you tell me about why you think Oren might be haunting the place, too? Or haunting you?" Uh oh. More napkin fluttering. "But only if you want to," I said hurriedly. "Otherwise, we can just tag all the stuff you'd like to move up to the attic and call it a day."

"No, I want to tell you. I want to *understand*." Another lift and drop of his shoulders, which I think were broader than they looked under his oversized cardigan. "We... we fought."

My fingers tensed on the china, and I carefully set it aside so I wouldn't be tempted to throw it. "Did he—" I swallowed, wrestling with that domestic violence trigger again. From all I'd heard about Oren, I didn't think he was an abuser, but I had to ask. "Did he hurt you? *Hit* you?"

"No! Never! I didn't mean— That's not—" He ran his hands through his hair and I noted that while he didn't always affect the real world—the cake, for instance—his transparent fingers disarranged his transparent hair, no problem. Maybe it was an etheric frequency thing? Who knew?

"Oren was in Toronto for a project. Had been for two months while the renovations were completed here, which, I have to admit, I was a little angry about. I mean, no, he'd done his part of the work with the design. The construction crew was responsible for executing it. But I missed him. And it was *our* house, now. I'd put him on the deed before we started the work.

And he'd known about the party for weeks. But he told me he couldn't make it. That he had to stay with the Toronto project until it was completed, and it would be at least another two weeks. I… yelled at him." His gaze dropped, and one napkin escaped. I flattened it to the table with my palm. "I told him I wouldn't reschedule the party. If he couldn't be bothered to show up, he could read about the good time we all had in *Boos News*. And then I hung up on him."

I winced. I knew all about angry words spoken in the heat of the moment, and the regrets that followed. "Was that the last time you spoke?"

"No. He gave me a little time to cool off and then he called me back right before I went to bed. He told me that he…" His voice choked, and he had to swallow. "That he understood. That he was sorry. But that he promised to make it up to me when he got home. He had a surprise for me, he said, and made me promise."

"Promise what?"

Avi lifted his chin to gaze at me, his expression bleak. "I promised to wait for him until he got home." The napkins flapped wildly. "I waited. I kept my promise. When will he keep his?"

The napkins made a break for it, and this time I didn't stop them.

Chapter Twenty-Three

After I let Avi express his feelings with paper goods, he calmed down, and we made a tour of the house so he could tag the things he wanted for his attic retreat. There were remarkably few things, and he seemed confused that some things he wanted weren't where he expected, although we usually found them elsewhere.

After we finished, he said good night to me outside the door of the main suite and vanished, so I took the rest of the evening to actually move into my room—put away my clothes, stow my toiletries in the bathroom, make the bed with the sheets I'd washed yesterday.

And let me tell you, a night on the most comfortable mattress I'd ever slept in made a huge difference in both my physical and mental wellbeing. I awoke early, totally refreshed, and had the rest of Sofia's cake for breakfast.

Hey. Don't judge until you've tried it.

I didn't see Avi before I left, and although we'd reached an understanding, I still dropped Gil off with Sofia, because until we figured out who Avi had detected, I wasn't willing to leave Gil trapped in there. While Avi could stuff keyholes with sawdust, he couldn't open the door to free Gil from any danger in the house, and I wouldn't want him wandering the neighborhood, anyway.

I got to the Manor at seven, apparently beating Saul to work since my Civic was the only car in the lot. I was glad for the extra uninterrupted time, because this morning, I had a second agenda, a personal one.

Thaddeus Richdale had spent practically his whole life immersed in his search for the supernatural. There must be something in his papers that detailed his actions and their results. Something I could use to understand what was going on with Avi.

I'd just started cataloging the first crate and its contents when my phone beeped. I wiped my dusty hands off on my jeans—too bad the Manor didn't have a spectral dust collection service like my house did, because it could really use it—and retrieved my phone from my jacket pocket.

"Hello?"

"Hey, Maz. It's Taryn. The delivery guys are ten minutes out from your place."

"Shoot. I'm not there. I came in to work early, but I can head back now."

She chuckled. "Don't stress. They'll no doubt stop in at Isaksen's on their way, so I'm sure they'll give you a few minutes' grace."

"Thanks, Taryn. I won't keep them waiting long."

I made sure to mark my place in the current dusty crate, and then ran back down to the car to head home. When I got there, Ricky was just stepping out of Sofia's door. He waved and headed over to meet me on my lawn.

"Morning," he said with a grin. "You're on the move early."

"Yeah. I've already been to work, but the delivery guys are on their way with Oren's effects, so I need to let them in."

"You know, if it's the guys from Transitions, I could probably get them to help me move Avi's things upstairs." He shrugged, tucking his thumbs in his jeans pockets. "If you're ready for that, I mean."

"We are, actually. We tagged everything he wanted last night. Look for the big neon orange dots." I grinned as a big panel truck with *Transitions Transportation* stenciled on the side turned down the street. "And it looks like you've got your muscle, too."

"Fantastic. We'll get this settled in no time."

But when the two delivery guys rolled up the truck's rear door with a rattle and boom, I wasn't so sure. Not only was the thing packed with boxes—and I mean *packed*—but there was furniture too.

"Wow. I didn't realize there'd be so *much*. I mean, he was essentially living here, right?"

"Not quite. He hadn't closed up his Portland house, so I guess this is everything from there plus his business," Ricky said. "Wonder who boxed it up?"

"Taryn mentioned an estate sale service," I said distractedly, as one delivery guy—whose name tag read Keegan—pulled out a metal ramp and let it bump onto the asphalt. "I guess they handled everything."

The second guy—Nando, according to his embroidered shirt—raised a hand to Ricky as he clanked up the ramp in his steel-toed boots. "Ricky. Qué pasa, man?"

"Estoy bien. But you won't be if you don't stop in and say hello to Tia before you leave." Ricky glanced at me. "We're cousins."

Nando grinned. "Second cousins. But don't worry. We'll be stopping by Tia's. I heard she made a tres leches cake yesterday."

I cleared my throat. "There, um, may not be much—"

Ricky elbowed me and gestured to the truck. "Need some help?"

"Wouldn't turn it down. What's the catch?"

"I've got some stuff to move up to the attic after you're done." Ricky raised an eyebrow at me. "How much are we talking?"

"Not a lot," I said. "And nothing too heavy."

"No problem." Nando smiled at me as Keegan wheeled a hand truck stacked with boxes down the ramp. He held out a hand for me to shake. "You must be Maz. Want to show Keegan where you'd like us to park this?"

"Uh, sure." I hustled up the flagstone path to where Keegan was positioning an adjustable ramp over the porch stairs. I dodged around him to unlock the door, giving Avi a mental thank you for not expressing his feelings with sawdust again, and Sofia for watching Gil. Pausing in the vestibule as Keegan wheeled in the first load, I eyed the boxes—they were the bankers' variety, so probably papers and books?

I pointed through the library's doors. "Why don't you drop those over there next to the dining room archway?"

"You got it." Keegan tipped the stack off the hand truck and headed back outside.

I peered out the open door at Ricky and Nando maneuvering an upholstered love seat down the ramp. There was *a lot* of stuff in that truck. The boxes alone might fill up the available space in the library. And the furniture… Would it upset Avi to see it all? I made a snap decision and hurried onto the porch.

"Hey, guys? Could we store this stuff in the basement, please?"

"You're the boss," Nando said. Then he cast a glance over his shoulder. "You gonna want to go through all these boxes down there, though?"

Hmmm. Good point. "How about this? All the furniture goes down there, but I've got a completely empty pantry. Let's put the boxes in there." The butler's pantry and kitchen cabinets had more than enough space for my food, once I had a chance to go shopping, and I could shut the door to the second pantry to shield the contents from Avi.

The guys were incredibly efficient and speedy once I got out of their way at their apologetic and polite request. I kept my eyes open for Avi sightings, but he didn't appear, not even when the guys carted his chosen stuff up to the attic. Between the furniture in the basement and the boxes stowed away in the pantry, I resigned myself to hours of sorting through Oren's possessions, which was only daunting because of the quantity. However, I hoped going through his belongings would help me know him better. In a way, this would be the same kind of project as my job with Thaddeus Richdale's effects at the Manor, although in Oren's case, there were people in town—heck, in my own house—who'd actually known him.

Keegan, Nando, and Ricky clattered down the stairs after their last trip to the attic, laughing and chatting. I met them in the entryway.

"I can't thank you enough, fellas. Do I owe you—"

"Nah." Nando waved a hand. "We're good. Taryn paid the bill already and Ricky's giving us a tip for the extra work." He patted his flat belly. "Lunch at Taqueria Vargas."

"Don't pretend you don't just want a chance to gossip with Felicia," Keegan said.

Nando snorted. "Like you don't?"

"Calm down, guys." Ricky turned to me. "We're heading to the restaurant after we stop in at Tia's. Will you join us?"

"I'd love to, but I'm kinda on the clock. I need to get back to the Manor and get something done today."

"What about dinner?"

Ricky's shy glance from under his lashes sent a little shiver up my spine, and you know what? Screw caution and my lousy romantic track record. No reward without risk, right?

"I'd like that. Seven? That'll give me a chance to shower the dust off."

His infectious grin bloomed. "You got it. See you then!"

"The truck okay parked at the curb for a while?" Keegan asked.

"Fine by me. I don't think there are any town ordinances that forbid it."

Ricky shook his head, so the guys locked up their truck and headed for Sofia's house while I waited on my porch. Just before they walked inside, Ricky looked over and waved. My answering wave was probably accompanied by a goofy smile.

But hey, can you blame me? A cute guy, a pending date, and a room that I'd been promised would remain completely private. Yeah, maybe I wouldn't move quite *that* fast, but the possibilities put a definite spring in my step when I returned to the Manor. In fact, I *may* have danced up the stairs—since nobody was there to see me, nobody could judge.

When my phone rang again, I was elbow deep in a crate layered with papers, random artifacts, and a metric ton of dust, so, after sneezing twice, I used a voice command to answer the call on speaker. "Hello?"

"Maz? Good morning. It's Carson."

"Oh, hi." I lifted a rosewood planchette with brass casters from a nest of muslin and set it aside carefully before grabbing a tissue and dabbing at my nose. "How are you?"

"Fine, fine. I was just wondering…" He laughed, a self-deprecating sound that surprised me for someone with Carson's polish. But then I remembered he'd taken some self-confidence hits as a kid, even if it had been distorted through a child's perception of rejection.

"Go ahead. Hit me." My voice was still thickened with dust. I should probably start wearing a mask for this job.

"Would you like to have dinner with me tonight?" he said in a rush. "I've got reservations at Maison Vallée in Richdale for eight."

Crap. Awkward. If I was sort of pursuing maybe-more-than-friendship with Ricky, I couldn't really lead Carson on. This was such a new experience for me. I'd rarely had one person interested in me, let alone two at once. "I'd, um, love to be friends, Carson, but if you were hoping for more, well… I'm kind of seeing somebody right now."

"Seeing someone?" His tone was decidedly tart. "Between yesterday and today?"

"Well. Yeah."

There was a beat of silence. "It's Ricky, isn't it?"

"I just want to be upfront with you, okay? And like I said, I'm happy to—"

"Sure. Right. See you around sometime."

"Carson, please don't—"

But he disconnected the call. I kicked myself for not handling that better. This was a small town, after all. I couldn't afford to alienate the residents. Although Carson didn't live here, did he?

Nevertheless, I didn't want to piss anybody off before I'd been here four whole days. That was a record even for me. On the other hand, accepting that no meant no was something everybody had to learn—and something I might have to embrace myself if Ricky's interest was strictly platonic.

The next thing I pulled out of the crate put Carson and Ricky completely out of my mind. Because underneath the crumpled muslin was a slim, leather-bound journal, secured with a faded blue ribbon. I carefully removed the ribbon and opened the little book. On the flyleaf, in perfect Victorian copperplate rendered in sepia ink, were words that made my mouth turn dry.

On Spiritus Communion

Observations by Frances Richdale

"Holy shit," I muttered. My hands were shaking so hard I had to set the journal aside lest I tear its pages. A first person account of paranormal experimentation at Richdale Manor. This was exactly what Saul had been hoping for—what *I'd* been hoping for, but for a different reason.

Saul wanted a clearer picture of the Manor's history. I wanted to help Avi. Don't get me wrong, I'm sure Saul wanted to help Avi too, since they'd been friends, but his motivation was colored by his ties with the Manor and Ghost's legacy.

Mine was more personal.

I had a grief-stricken dead guy living in the house with me and I wanted to make him happy. Happi*er*. Or at least more comfortable.

My hands were besmirched with dust, so before I touched the journal again, I raced for the bathroom, scrubbed my hands, and blotted them dry on the embroidered hand towel Saul had left for me.

I crept back to the document room as though I were stalking a skittish Gil before a vet visit. The journal was right where I left it, of course, so I reverently lifted it and sank down in the chair again, hoping that against all the Victorian-era odds, Frances Richdale was clear-eyed, clear-headed, and thorough.

She'd drawn the line on *Heliotrope*, anyway, so I could be forgiven for having reasonable expectations about her intelligence and fortitude.

I inhaled deeply and exhaled between pursed lips before turning to the first page and beginning to read.

Whereas my Husband has devoted all our Resources to his Pursuits, it behooves me to chronicle his Actions, ere he once again repeat failed Trials to no avail and to the great detriment of our Family's wealth and well-being.

Hot *damn*, but Frances Richdale was the shit.

Grinning, I kept reading, enjoying Frances's acerbic commentary about Thaddeus's increasingly desperate attempts more than the accounts of the experiments themselves. Not because the explanations were poor. Far from it. Frances was meticulous in her descriptions, covering not only the steps Thaddeus employed, but also the date of the attempt, the weather, the room—its relative heat, its furnishings, and how they differed from previous trails—the other participants, their attitudes, and of course, the results.

Which were always failures.

I suspect Frances kept such detailed records so she could prove to Thaddeus that he'd done the same thing before, without success. Unfortunately, that may have backfired on her, because as time went on, armed with her comprehensive reports, Thaddeus began tweaking one tiny item at a time.

"Maz?" Saul's voice from the doorway made me fumble the journal, but I managed to catch it before fell. "Sorry, I didn't mean to startle you, but it's past six." He chuckled. "I admire your dedication, but there's no time limit on this project."

"Past six? Crap!" I glanced around frantically for something to mark my place before spotting the blue ribbon that had bound the journal. "I've got a date at seven."

Saul made that shooing motion again. "Then get moving. Maybe tomorrow you can fill me in on what you found that's so fascinating. I'll lock up here."

"Absolutely." I grabbed my jacket. "Thanks, Saul. See you tomorrow!"

I jetted out of the Manor and zoomed out of the lot in a spray of gravel. When I got to my place, the Transitions Transportation truck was gone. I pulled the Civic into the garage and ran for the mud room entrance as the garage door trundled down behind me, shrugging out of my jacket as I ran.

The instant I stepped inside, though, Avi popped in front of me, eyes wild. "Someone was here."

"Yeah, I know." I dodged around him and hung my jacket on a hook. "The delivery guys. They helped Ricky move all your stuff up to the attic."

"Not *them*," Avi snapped. "Somebody else."

"A-another ghost?" Fear clawed at my belly, but can you blame me? I'd spent all afternoon reading about all the ways people *failed* to reach a ghost, and I had not one but possibly two successes but had no idea *why*.

"Possibly. I don't know." When he motioned for me to follow, his arm passed through mine, making me shiver. He took off through the kitchen, and man, he could really *move* because I had to run to keep up. He stopped outside the library doors and pointed inside, his faded body glitching like a spliced videotape.

"Not the library," I muttered as I slowed. "Not again." I peeked inside, expecting the shower of books. But instead, every single one of Oren's boxes was upended, their contents strewn over the floor.

"This time," Avi said, flickering like a strobe light, "I know it wasn't me."

I glanced through him at the front door. It was ajar, although I could have sworn I locked it behind me, but I'd been distracted by Ricky, so maybe I'd forgotten.

"I believe you." I pushed the door closed, hearing the latch click. "But I don't think it was another ghost either. This time, somebody actually broke in. The question is, what are they looking for?"

Chapter Twenty-Four

I didn't waste any time calling the ghost posse. I'd promised, after all.

"Hey, Saul. It's Maz. There's been another incident here at the house."

"Another manifestation?" Saul's voice practically quivered with excitement, although I caught the sound of another voice in the background.

"Maybe. Well, I mean Avi's here, but we're not sure about the source of the… interference. Should I call Professor DeHaven too?"

"Don't bother. She's teaching tonight. I'll fill her in on our investigation later."

That other voice—which I assumed was Jerry—said something else I couldn't catch, and Saul, clearly responding to Jerry, not me, said, "It will only take a few minutes." Another muffled response. "All right, no more than an hour, I promise. Maz?"

"Still here."

"I'll be right there."

"Great. See you soon."

Then I texted Ricky, since our date was about to be collateral damage. His response—*OMW*—was immediate. Avi was still staring at the library, wringing his hands, so I approached him slowly.

"Hey. Saul and Ricky will be here shortly. We'll get everything sorted."

He didn't look at me. "Will we? How?"

Hunh. Good question. "I don't know for sure, but I know we'll try. Until they arrive, though, why not go upstairs for a bit?"

He slid me a sideways glance. "Afraid I'll go poltergeist on you and make things worse?"

"No. But nothing will happen until Saul gets here, so take a little time for yourself, okay? Time enough to face the… the…" I flipped off the mess in the library. "The latest *invasion* when we've got backup."

Avi hesitated for an instant, but then nodded. "Perhaps you're right."

"Every once in a while, I manage. But Avi?"

"Yes?"

"You're not alone."

He met my gaze, and his expression softened. "Neither are you." Then he vanished.

As a result, I was standing at the library doors, scowling at the second coming of chaos, when Ricky knocked.

I opened the door and motioned him inside. "Hi. Sorry, but I guess I'll be taking another raincheck on dinner."

"Forget apologies." He stepped across the threshold and took my hands. "Are you okay?"

I heaved a sigh. "I'm more okay than Avi." I angled my head toward the paper pile. "I've only got sorting and cleanup ahead of me, but he's really upset about somebody violating his space again. It's bad enough that he's had a new random roommate foisted on him without his consent."

"Hey." Ricky squeezed my hands. "I think he's probably grateful for you. After all, you're the only one who can see him. The only one who's looking out for him. It was your idea to trick out the attic for him, after all."

"I guess." I pulled Ricky farther into the vestibule as Saul charged up the walk.

"What did I miss?" Saul was out of breath, but his blue eyes sparkled. "Is it another entity? Do you think this house might be a gateway?"

I shivered. "Crap, that's all we'd need. But no. I'm pretty sure we're talking about a corporeal vandal this time."

Saul visibly drooped. "Are you sure?" When I nodded, he muttered, "Drat."

"The only thing I'm marginally certain about is that they left through the front door because it wasn't latched. And whoever —"

"Or *whatever*," Saul said.

Gee, thanks for that, Saul. Nevertheless, I inclined my head. "Or whatever it was, they were super focused on the boxes clearly labeled as Oren's. It doesn't appear that anything else was disturbed."

"Really?" Ricky frowned as he let go of my right hand, although he didn't release my left. "How can you tell?"

I huffed a strangled laugh, as much from the continued contact as the question. "A point."

"If it was another ghost, though," Ricky said, "wouldn't you have been able to detect it?"

"Why would I?" I flailed my free hand. "I'm not the freaking ghost whisperer. I'm not sure why I can see Avi. I mean, nobody else can."

"Right, right." Ricky released my hand. "Sorry."

"No." I sighed and laced our fingers together again. "*I'm* sorry. But having our house trashed multiple times is getting a little old." Ricky gave me a weird look. "What?"

"You said *our house*."

I blinked. "Yeah, I guess I did." But since Avi was here first—and still was—it seemed presumptuous not to recognize his ownership. Besides, hadn't we just decided we were in this together?

"I don't mean to rush you, Maz," Saul said, "but I promised my husband I'd return soon enough for us to make it to the theater on time." He smiled, his lean cheeks pinking. "It's our anniversary."

"Oh. Yes. Sorry." I backed up, drawing Ricky with me, and gestured to the library. "Behold the incident."

Saul stared at the room, his eyebrows lifting. "Oh, my."

"Yeah. Avi met me at the mudroom door to tell me about this."

"He's not responsible for it?" Saul asked.

"He says not, and I believe him. He's really upset. I sent him upstairs to the attic to calm down."

Saul frowned. "Why would the attic calm him down?"

"We moved—that is, Ricky and the Transitions guys moved—some of the things he wanted up there so he can have a more comfortable, private space."

Saul cocked his head. "How do you know what he wanted?"

"He told me."

"He… told you. When?" Saul almost sounded hurt, as though I'd had a party and not invited him.

"Last night, after you all left."

"Ah. Of course."

"Although it's odd. It's as though he doesn't have much object permanence. He can't remember everything that ought to be here, but he recognizes important things when he sees them."

"In other words," Saul said, "when we were touring the house after Avi detected the intruder, if something *were* missing, he wouldn't have known."

"I hadn't thought of that." I glanced around the room, realizing that there had been remarkably few personal items in the house. Paintings, yes. Throw pillows, baskets, kitchenware, sheets, towels, blankets. Furniture. But no photographs. No tchotchkes or memorabilia. Nothing that would identify the people who had lived here as anything other than a couple who knew how to remodel and decorate. I turned to Ricky. "When you were here before, working for Avi and Oren, did they have personal items around? Pictures, knickknacks, mementos, anything like that?"

Ricky frowned. "Yeah. Mostly Avi's stuff, since Oren was holding off shipping his things until after the remodel was done."

"You see any around here?"

He pivoted slowly in place, scanning the shelves. "Now that you mention it, no."

"Where do you suppose it all went? Did someone come in after Avi's death to box things up?"

Saul shook his head. "No. Oren was adamant that everything remain as it was. As their attorney, I locked up everything myself."

I spotted what looked like an upside-down picture frame under a fan of papers in the corner and edged over to it. I picked it up and turned it over. It was a picture of two men, one of them clearly Avi, standing on the sidewalk under the maple tree, the house in the background. He was smiling at the camera, joy practically radiating off of him. The other man was a little older, his dark hair silvering at the temples. He was smiling too, but not at the camera. Instead, he was gazing down at Avi with such a tender expression that tears prickled in my eyes.

"That's Avi and Oren, the day they added Oren to the deed and changed both their wills in the other's favor," Saul said. "I took that picture myself and sent it to both of them."

Oren. He looked… lovely. My throat closed and I blinked rapidly, a hollow in my chest. I'd never had a chance to know him, never *would* get that chance. He'd never known me, and yet he'd left me this house and all his worldly possessions.

And also apparently Avi, his unworldly… Well, not possession, no. His *person*. The center of his life.

I made a silent vow to myself right then that whatever happened, I'd be the best steward of the house, of Oren's legacy, that I could be, and that included looking out for Avi. I set the picture in an empty spot at eye level on the nearest shelf.

"You know," Ricky said, "whoever ransacked these boxes was looking for something. I suspect that the wreck they made in here was because they were in a hurry, not because they were angry."

My eyes widened. "Shit! The pantry!"

Chapter Twenty-Five

I charged down the hall, the slap of my Converse changing tone as I pounded past the hardwood in the family room to the kitchen tiles. The pantry door was still closed. I reached out and grabbed the doorknob, murmuring, "Please, please, please," as I opened it slowly. I blew out a relieved breath, because the boxes inside were untouched.

Saul peered over my shoulder. "You store boxes in the pantry? Who stores boxes in the pantry?"

"Hey, it was available empty space." I smiled at him, a little crookedly. "Think of the Manor. In the original plans you showed me, the document room used to be the third parlor." I closed the door and patted one of its panels. "I'll have to go through all of this eventually, so I wanted them convenient, but out of the way. The basement seemed a little too far to— The basement! The furniture!"

I peeled out of the kitchen into the mudroom and clattered down the basement stairs, Ricky at my heels, with Saul following at a more measured pace.

I hadn't been down here after the Transitions guys finished unloading everything, but I'm pretty sure they wouldn't have knocked over a drafting table and opened a wooden chest, scattering its contents over the concrete floor around it. Every drawer on a wide flat file cabinet hung open, one actually yanked all the way out, with blueprints, renderings, and drafting tools appearing to have exploded out of it.

As I was attempting to force air into my lungs, Ricky reached out and tentatively touched my forearm.

"Maz. Nando and Keegan didn't do this. They wouldn't."

"I know." I gripped the stair railing, as though that would help me get hold of the emotions roiling in my chest. I wasn't even sure what they were at the moment. Rage was definitely a part of it. A little relief that they hadn't been more destructive, since even though the furniture—a leather sofa, a brocade loveseat, a cherrywood console table—had been disarranged, it hadn't been destroyed.

I spotted one pencil that had been snapped in half and identified another part of the emotional cocktail being shaken, not stirred, inside me.

Fear.

Because whoever had been here—whatever they'd been looking for—they were really freaking angry about not finding it.

"Do you suppose…" I had to clear my throat when my voice broke. "Do you think they found what they were after?"

"It's hard to say," Saul said. "Are you concerned with what might have been taken?"

"What? No. Heck, if I knew what it was, I'd probably tie it up with a bow and leave it on the porch." I spread my arms. "All of this—the house, its contents, Oren's things—is all a gift to me. I can't miss something I never had to begin with. What's more important is the security of the house, and the safety of everyone in it. Gil. Me. Avi. Things? Things they can have, unless they're something that has an emotional value to Avi."

"How will you know?" Saul asked. "You said he couldn't remember possessions unless he saw them."

I grimaced. "Yeah, there's that." Plus, seeing Oren's things desecrated might reignite his grief.

Saul made an apologetic noise. "I'm truly sorry to leave you with this, but I really do have to get back home if I don't want to be sleeping on the sofa on my anniversary."

"Oh, jeez." I shooed him up the stairs. "Go, go. This isn't anything you signed up for, Saul. Thanks for coming, but there's no reason for you to stay. Happy anniversary. You and Jerry have fun and enjoy your show."

"I'll let myself out, then. See you tomorrow?"

"You bet."

After Saul retreated upstairs, I gazed morosely at the disorder below me. "I suppose I should start cleaning things up."

"I'm not sure that's the best idea."

I glanced up at Ricky. "Why not?"

"I know you don't have any ideas about what could be missing, but since we're pretty sure this is a mundane break-in, you should at least report it to the police and leave everything untouched until they've had a chance to investigate. If this is a trend—"

"You mean a trend of my library getting paper piled?"

"No, I mean a burglary trend in Ghost."

I raised my eyebrows. "Ghost has a burglary trend?"

Ricky shrugged. "Maybe not a trend, per se, but things were taken from Tia's house a couple of months ago."

"Someone broke into Sofia's house?" At the thought of Sofia in danger, the fear and rage bubbled up again. "While she was home?"

"No. She was helping out at the restaurant at the time, trying to convince my mother to spice up the salsa." His mouth twisted in clear exasperation. "It wasn't technically a break-in anyway, since she never locks her doors. They didn't trash anything, but they took her TV. Some jewelry and cash, too, which she probably wouldn't even have noticed for weeks, except she wanted to loan Felicia a pair of earrings for her prom and the jewelry box was gone."

"If they're looking for cash here, they've come to the wrong house. But you're right. As much as it irks me to leave everything in this state, I should probably report this, if only for the insurance." I slapped my forehead. "Insurance. Crap. Do I even *have* insurance? If they've been looking for me for months —"

"Calm down." Ricky, half a head taller than me while standing a step above me, patted my shoulder. "I'm sure Taryn has it covered. She never misses details like that."

"Whew. Okay, then." I pulled out my phone, but hesitated. This wasn't an emergency, so 9-1-1 would be inappropriate, not for a cold burglary with no apparent property damage—if I didn't count the broken pencil. "Uh…"

Ricky chuckled softly and held out his hand. "I'll call the sheriff, if you like. They know me."

I handed over the phone. "Why do they know you? Because of Sofia's break-in?"

"No. Because one of my cousins works at the office."

"Exactly how many cousins do you have?"

"A lot." He didn't even look at the phone screen as he keyed in the number. "Catholic, remember? My great-grandparents each had seven siblings. It ballooned from— Hey, Yaz, it's me. No, it's a business call this time, so don't give me grief for calling you at work."

I followed him up the stairs as he outlined the details to his cousin. First thing tomorrow? I was contacting a security company and getting an alarm system installed, because I was *done* with people invading our home. How to pay for it could be an issue. Maybe Saul would give me an advance, or I could work out a payment plan with the security company. Or both. Both were probably in the cards.

When I reached the kitchen, Ricky was just disconnecting the call. He held out my phone with an apologetic shrug. "They'll send somebody out, but not until tomorrow, probably. There was a fire in Richdale. Possible arson, so all the on-duty deputies are on site with the fire department."

"No worries. It's not like any of this is going anywhere." I sighed. "Although, just in case, I should stick around. Which means no dinner date. Sorry."

He gave me a mock affronted stare. "Perdóname, but who do you think you are talking to? I'll hustle over to the restaurant and bring something back for both of us."

"You don't have to do that. I'll be—" The loud rumble of my stomach made Ricky grin. "Okay, you got me. That sounds great."

"Good. Any preferences?"

"Everything's been wonderful so far, so surprise me?"

He nodded. "I'll collect Gil from Tia's on the way back, too."

"I can—"

"Maz." He rested his hand on my shoulder. "Let me do these things for you, all right?"

My shoulders slumped, a release of the muscles in my back and neck that had been tensed since I walked in the door. "I should probably protest more, but—"

"Don't. Please."

"I won't. I don't have the slightest inclination. So I'll just say thank you. Sincerely."

"Hey." One side of his mouth lifted in a lopsided smile. "What are friends for?"

Friends. Right. Friends.

I followed him down the hall. After I closed the front door behind him, I took a moment to lean my forehead against the smooth, cool wood. "Man, this has been a day."

I shuffled out of the entryway, but when I passed the library doors, I spotted Avi inside. He was standing by the shelf, gazing at the photograph of him and Oren, not glitching anymore.

"I remember this photo," he said as he ran a finger across its face. "Saul took it."

"Yes. He told us." I stepped inside, careful to steer clear of everything on the floor. "The day you put Oren on the deed."

"We were so happy. We asked Saul to make us both a copy, so we'd remember while we went through the renovation." He laughed softly. "Oren said we needed it to remind us, because renovation was such a stressful process and a lot of couples lost sight of the reason they were going through that particular hell. To have a home. To be together. To start a life."

"This was Oren's copy. Do you know where yours could be? I haven't seen it anywhere."

Avi blinked at me. "I…" He walked to the center of the room, feet flowing through the mess as though he were wading through a creek—a creek made of paper—although of course he didn't damage or displace anything. Once there, he turned in a circle, studying the shelves much as Ricky had done. "It should have been here. A lot of things should have been here. I don't understand— Oh!" His troubled expression cleared. "I remember. I'd moved everything so I could rearrange the books. I didn't put anything back because I wanted Oren and I to decorate the space them together."

"Where did you put them in the meantime?" There hadn't been any boxes or crates in the house until Oren's effects were delivered.

"The window seats, of course."

"Window seats?"

He pointed to the bank of windows in the corner. "We built them into all the turrets." He wrinkled his nose. "Sue me. I read *Jane Eyre* in junior high."

"You, too?" I said. "Window seats are the *best*." For a moment, we shared a smile—just two guys who dug window seats.

"The only thing I took away from that book—other than Jane needed a serious fashion intervention—was that when I had a house of my own, it would have window seats *everywhere*."

Although… "There's no window seat in the attic."

Avi shrugged. "The turrets only have two floors and we decided to spare the kitchen in favor of seating with actual backs. Oren offered to put them in the third floor dormers, but I told him that could wait, since we weren't really planning to spend any time up there. He still included them in all the plans.

Future expansion, he called it. A hangout for our kids when they discovered *Jane Eyre*."

His gaze drifted to the photograph and right then, I made a decision: As soon as I had more than grocery money—and once the security system was paid for—those dormers were getting window seats.

"Although, since Oren was way more practical than me, he turned all of them into storage chests. Go on. Look."

Chapter Twenty-Six

I skirted the room, staying close to the bookshelves since I didn't share Avi's non-corporeal non-weight and wanted to leave the scene more or less intact for the deputies when they finally arrived. While the graceful curved desk took up a third of the turret, the other two-thirds were lined with what I'd assumed were simply upholstered benches. Window seats, sure, but when I'd tried to lift them to see if there was anything underneath, they hadn't budged. I tried again. No luck.

"You have to slide them forward before you lift the lid," Avi said. "Oren didn't want us to have to remove the cushions to open the chests, so he did this thing—don't ask me what it's called—to make it work."

"Clever," I said, hooking my fingers under the overhang of the first window seat. Sure enough, I felt a subtle groove under the lip and pulled. It glided forward for two or three inches—the depth of the cushion—then lifted easily before locking in place.

Avi pointed at the hinges. "Oren installed those so the lid wouldn't fall down and bonk you on the head as you rummaged around." He rubbed the back of his head as he said this, and I wondered if he remembered his injury.

Then I actually could hear his breath catch, which was a first. Mine did too, for that matter. Because the window seat was *packed*. Don't get me wrong—it wasn't a rat's nest. Everything was arranged neatly and carefully padded if necessary, from photographs to knickknacks to Avi's framed diploma from the

University of Oregon. But what Avi's gaze was riveted on was a porcelain bowl that almost glowed in the twilight, nestled in a soft-looking red knitted *something,* although I couldn't tell if it was a scarf or a sweater. The bowl's inner walls were white, with a sinuous crimson dragon chasing its tail just under the rim.

Avi knelt down and touched the fabric. "I was wearing this sweater the first time I met Oren. It was at Reminiscence."

"Reminiscence?"

He didn't look away from the sweater. "The second-hand store in town. The owner has great taste, so she only stocks things that are beautiful or functional, even if they're not quite antiques. Oren was working on the B&B renovation and he was scouting for room decorations. He'd identified this bowl as being perfect for their bridal suite, but I'd wandered by and picked it up before he could bring the owners back to see it." Avi looked up at me, eyes swimming with ghostly tears. "He bought it for me instead, because the dragon matched the sweater."

I had to swallow a couple of times before I could speak. "Would you like to have it in your attic?"

"I… Yes. Yes, please."

"You got it. If you see anything else you want, just say the word and I'll take it upstairs." He nodded, but didn't move, and I gave myself a mental facepalm. *He can't lift anything.* "Do you want me to unpack everything so you can decide?"

He lifted one shoulder. "Maybe later." He glanced up at me. "Could you leave this one for now? You can go ahead and look in the other seats if you want, but I… need a minute."

"Sure. No problem." I moved to the farthest seat, the one that abutted the desk, to give him at least a semblance of privacy. The lid didn't open quite as smoothly as the first one, seeming to catch on something that required me to tug a little harder. As soon as I locked the hinges, I could see why.

Although most of the contents were arranged as neatly as in the first chest, there was a chenille throw jammed into the front right corner. Something was shoved upside down into the throw, and its base—at least two inches thick and as wide as my palm—extended above the lip of the chest, enough to have scored the underside of the lid.

Well, *that* wouldn't do. I didn't want anything to damage our window seats, even if the damage couldn't be seen.

So I grabbed it, but *dang*, this thing was *heavy*, the base's edges sharp against my palm. Whatever stood atop it—or underneath it, I suppose, considering its current orientation—snagged on the chenille as I lifted.

Fuzz *floofed* around me as I disengaged the throw, because the main body of the thing, glinting with gold between the loose-knit chenille, had more spiky parts than a tumbleweed.

"Ha! Got you," I muttered as I finally freed it. I draped the throw over the open lid because I needed both hands to turn the thing right side up.

And nearly dropped it on my foot. Because I recognized the stack of books rising for over ten inches, graduating from the fully open one at the bottom to the completely closed one at the top, like some exotic, angular flower.

The Lang Literary Award.

Snippets of conversations since I'd arrived in Ghost sparked in my memory like fireflies. Avi was a writer. I'd been told that more than once, but I'd never asked for any details, not even from Avi himself.

But this… Avi wasn't just a writer. He was a *writer.* A writer who was good enough to win one of the most prestigious awards in all of genre fiction. My hands shook as I edged toward the desk to set it down. And nearly dropped it again when I read the brass plaque on the base.

Lang Literary Award 2004

Presented to Jake Fields

"What the…" I croaked.

I must have sounded sufficiently peculiar to catch Avi's attention because even though he didn't shift his focus from the bowl and sweater, he asked, "You all right?"

"You're Jake Fields?"

"Mmmhmm."

"You're Jake Fields."

"Yes. Or at least I was."

"You're *Jake Fields*."

"I *said*—" He sat back on his heels and looked up at me, but when his gaze flicked to what I was holding, his face screwed up in disgust. "Oh. That."

I brandished it. "Yes. This. You won the freaking *Lang*, Avi. 2004… that must have been for *Behind Time*, right? I remember because I thought it was so well-deserved. Why would you shove it upside down in a window seat?"

He scowled. "Because it was *mocking* me. I was getting absolutely nowhere with the next book. It was nothing but drivel."

"Drivel." I stared down at him. "That's the first word you said to me. Drivel."

"Maybe because it's what I'd been saying to myself for weeks. I'd gotten to about chapter four and then everything turned dead and dull." He sat back and folded his arms around his knees. "I think I was trying to force it, you know? I was missing Oren, and wanted to get the book to my agent before he got back, and instead I couldn't make any headway at all." His brow pleated. "I must have fallen asleep at the desk, because I woke up with that thing staring at me. I was so irritated that I just shoved it into the chest to get it out of my sight."

"When was this?"

"I don't know. A couple of days before the party?"

My scalp prickled and those damn spectral spiders staged another curtain call down my back. I peered closely at the base of the award and saw a discoloration on one corner. I held it away from my body.

"Holy crap." I tiptoed to the desk and set it gingerly in the center of the blotter. "I need to call Jerry. Or the police. Or Jerry and the police."

"What in the world for?"

"Because..." I swallowed and wiped my hands on my jeans at the thought that my fingerprints might have just contaminated the evidence. "Because I think this might be the murder weapon."

"Murder weapon? Whose murder?"

"Well." I met his gaze. "Yours."

Chapter Twenty-Seven

Avi stared at me, mouth agape. "Wait. I was *murdered*?"

I winced. *Shit.* We hadn't really talked about *Avi's* death, had we? This probably wasn't the best way to break the news. "Maybe?"

Oren's either, other than he was gone, and when I came to think about it, I'd never asked about Oren's manner of death either. I made a mental note to ask Taryn, if only so I could share that information with Avi. When he was ready. When he *asked*.

Which wasn't right now.

I hunkered down, putting myself on his eye level, wondering briefly whether he could float. *Not relevant now, Maz.*

"Hey. I'm sorry. I should have broken that to you a little better. But to be honest, I assumed you knew."

His face bunched as though he were trying to peer through fog. "Why?"

"Because I like you, of course. I don't want to make you unhappy. More unhappy."

He made an impatient gesture with one hand. "I'm not talking about your tact or lack of it. Why would you assume I knew I was murdered?"

I blinked at that. "Because you were there?"

His expression morphed into one of clear exasperation. "Maz. I haven't remembered the most important things in my *life*"—his gaze cut to the bowl—"until they're right in front of me. I didn't even know I *was* dead until you told me. Why would you think I could remember anything about how I got…" He flailed. "*Here*? Like this?"

"Okay. Then let's think about that." I folded my legs under me and sat facing him. "What's the last thing you remember?"

He gnawed on his lower lip, squinting at the ceiling. "I only really remember… waiting. For Oren to come back, like he promised." He met my eyes, smiling crookedly. "You probably know more about it than I do, since you have the benefit of the police investigation."

I scratched the back of my head. "Weeelll…"

His smile faded and his eyes narrowed. "Didn't they find the perpetrator?"

"They sort of… didn't look."

"Didn't look? I was killed and they didn't even…" His face crumpled. "Not even Oren?"

I reached out, but of course my hand passed right through his arm, so I drew back. "They didn't look because they didn't know. The cause of death was a subdural hematoma, and you collapsed in the backyard during the party, in front of practically the whole town. As far as anybody knew, it was from natural causes." I gripped a handful of my curls and yanked. "Jeez, I'm not handling this well at all."

"No. No, it's all right." Avi straightened his shoulders, making an obvious attempt to pull himself together. "As long as it wasn't just indifference. As long as Oren wasn't… Oh, god. Oren. He must have been—"

"Devastated. That's why he never came back to the house. He couldn't face the place without you. He had Saul lock it up."

"Then why do you think I was murdered?"

"Jerry was suspicious. He's the one who thought you might have been subject to prior head trauma."

"You'd think I'd remember getting hit in the head hard enough to *kill* me," Avi said tartly. I looked pointedly at the bowl. "Yeah, yeah. Memory not firing on all cylinders, so maybe I wouldn't."

"Do you remember anything more about the day of the party? After you stuffed the Lang in the window seat?"

"I remember…" His gaze turned distant. "Oh! I remember I had a headache, because I promised myself I'd take a couple of ibuprofen before the party, as soon as I finished the chapter."

"Were you writing on a laptop?"

He shook his head. "I didn't have a laptop, just a monitor and an internet-connected keyboard."

I'd seen those tucked into a closet upstairs, along with a printer, and had wondered about the absence of a CPU. "Ah."

"At the time, though, I was using the typewriter, because the change in haptics, the typebars hitting the paper? Well, it was better for releasing aggression when I was blocked." He huffed a little laugh. "Although I'm surprised I'm here now instead of the circle of hell reserved for environmental destroyers because I'd filled the wastebasket with page after page of junk. I'd just dumped all four completed chapters in there too because it clearly wasn't working."

Hmmm… Although the floor was awash in paper—Oren's papers, this time—the black mesh trash basket was empty. Avi seemed to have a certain… affinity with paper, bringing the total of things he could manipulate to three, along with dust and sawdust, so I had to ask.

"Did you, um, *poof* the trash like you did the dust?"

"What, with a wiggle of my nose or a wave of my wand? I was planning to give everyone a tour of the completed renovations during the party. I wouldn't have wanted the evidence of my failure there for all to see. I probably emptied it beforehand."

"Do you remember if it was full?"

He glared at me irritably. "Maz, I never remembered ordinary housework when I was alive. What makes you think I can remember it now? All I know is that the book wasn't working. Now that I'm thinking about it, that was probably because I was mad at Oren, so even though Harcourt and Corchran were supposed to be cooperating to track down a serial kidnapper, they kept bickering like a couple of *Real Housewives*."

I practically choked on my own spit. After I stopped coughing, I wheezed, "Wait. What?"

Avi shrugged. "I know. Totally out of character for them." While I was still trying to catch my breath, he turned his head and ran a finger along the edge of the bowl again. "I never expected Corchran to have such a big a footprint in the series, but then I met Oren and he sort of *became* Corchran in *Behind Time* just because I wanted to spend more time with him, even if only on paper."

"Uh…"

"My agent was in talks with HBO on a Harcourt series. If it had ever gone forward, my dream casting for Corchran was John Barrowman."

I managed to find my voice. "Good choice. And he turned into the most drool-worthy silver fox you've ever seen."

Avi's eyes practically lit up. "Really? That would have been even more perfect, since Oren was already starting to go prematurely gray. People had been talking about the unresolved sexual tension between Harcourt and Corchran since *Bullseye*, and I was determined to finally let them bang it out in this book. But"—he spread his hands, palms up—"bickering. Petty on-page bickering. Not something befitting a tough-as-nails PI and reformed master thief."

"Yeah, I can see that. But getting them together would have been impossible, anyway. Hell, the bickering was impossible."

He rolled his eyes. "I *know*. That's not how they operate. Either of them."

"Not because it's out of character." I forced a breath into my leaden lungs. "Because Corchran is dead."

Avi stared at me, open-mouthed, for a good ten seconds. "What are you talking about? Corchran isn't dead."

I nodded slowly. "Sorry, but he is. Don't you remember? You killed him in the last book."

Chapter Twenty-Eight

"*What?*"

I had my answer to my question about Avi floating, because with that shout, he levitated almost to the ceiling. The papers behind him started to rustle before they lifted into the air and began to circle the room.

"Avi. Please. We're disturbing the crime scene."

"I didn't kill Corchran. I would *never* kill Corchran. Corchran was *Oren*. Harcourt was going to *propose* to him if I— If they— Gah!" He clutched his hair with both hands and the paper picked up speed. "Why would you think I would *kill* him?"

I scrambled to my feet, which put my head about level with his loafers. "If you come back down, we can talk about it, okay?"

He glared down at me, eyes practically glowing, and for a moment, all I could think was, *oh, shit*. True, Avi had never flung anything but paper around, but I'd read *Cards as Weapons*. Paper could be *lethal*, and death by a thousand paper cuts was *not* the way I wanted to go.

I throttled back on my flight reflex, though, because despite Carson's claims of unspecified childhood emotional abuse, I didn't think Avi was homicidal. I kept my voice level. Calm but firm. Ish.

"How about you let everything settle and we can figure things out, all right? You don't want to trash Oren's stuff, do you?"

Avi froze for an instant and then glanced behind him. He let go of his hair, but his fingers still curled into fists, his chest heaving, so I wasn't sure if he was winding up for an explosion or backing away from the edge. After another few seconds, he returned to the floor, although it was more of a flop than a float. The paper followed suit. But while it stopped, Avi kept going until he was crumpled in a heap next to the window seat.

When I sat down beside him, he raised his head and gazed at me, and I was rocked back from the total devastation in his expression.

"Avi..."

"I would never kill Corchran. You have to believe me."

"I believe that's what *you* believe, at least now. But *Borderline* has been out for three years."

His brows drew together, and the grief was replaced by something I couldn't quite identify. "*Borderline*? What are you talking about?"

"*Borderline* was the last Ziv Harcourt book."

"No. It wasn't."

"Yeah. It was." I took a fortifying breath. "Fans had been waiting for it for six years, so we all jumped on it as soon as it hit the shelves."

"And I'm telling you no. The last Harcourt and Corchran book was *All In*."

It was my turn to frown. "*All In*? That's not—"

"The identity theft case? Harcourt's sister being gaslighted by her loser husband? Harcourt and Corchran going undercover at the spa?"

"Uh..."

"The mud bath scene? Oh, come *on*, you *must* remember the mud bath scene. Unless..." He scrubbed his hands over his face. Was it weird that I was getting used to being able to see the room through him? "Oh god. You're not a Jake Fields reader. Sorry. I—"

"No! I'm totally a Jake Fields fan. But none of those things happened in *Borderline*."

"There. Was. No. Borderline," Avi shouted, and the edges of a good half of the papers started to flutter. "The last completed book was *All In,* but I hadn't turned it in to my agent yet because I wanted Oren to read it first, even before Patrice, and he hadn't had a chance because of the Toronto project and moving and he probably *lost* the manuscript while he was packing anyway because he never said a single thing about it in any of our calls. The only thing that was *borderline* was the stupid WIP that refused to cooperate. I actually changed the working title to *Borderline Garbage,* because that's what it was."

My ears rang as though someone had conked *me* with the Lang, because *holy shit,* was *that* was this was about? I lifted a finger. "One moment, okay? Just, um, hold that thought."

I scrambled to my feet and crossed to the desk. The top few pages of Patrice's neat pile of the deconstructed *Borderline* were askew from Avi's latest paper maelstrom, but it was mostly intact. I grabbed the stack and plopped back down, facing Avi.

"Take a look at this."

He reared back, revulsion flickering across his face. "What is that?"

"This is the only thing you've truly destroyed since I arrived."

"I'm sorry. I don't know why I did that. I've never destroyed a book before in my life. I don't remember doing it *now*."

"Maybe it was instinct." I lifted the title page and showed it to him. "*Borderline*. By Jake Fields."

"No." He tried to snatch it from me, and while he didn't manage to grasp it, it did flutter in my hand. "No no no no no."

Oren's papers started to make a break for it again. "Avi, I know you're not happy about this, but do you think you could maybe *target* the paper levitation a bit?"

"What?" He tried to grab the page again.

I set the whole stack on the floor, oriented toward him. "If you can flip over one at a time, you can read the book even if you can't hold it in your hands."

He pressed his lips together, throat working, but he nodded and focused on the pages in front of him. At first, he was only able to scatter them like they'd been hit by a wind gust, but after a few minutes of strain that brought out ghostly perspiration on his forehead, he gained enough control to be able to manipulate one page at a time.

As soon as he read the opening paragraph of the first chapter, his breath hitched. "This is…" Another few pages fluttered away. Then a few more. Then he lifted his chin and met my eyes. "These are the chapters I was working on before I— Word for word, Maz. Word for fucking *word*."

"You only got to about chapter four, right?"

"Halfway through five, actually."

"Check out six." Or maybe not. Six opened with the news of Corchran's death. "Ten. Check out chapter ten."

He nodded and bent over the book again, his forehead knotted as he concentrated on paper domination.

"So, Avi."

"Hmmm?"

"Who knew you were Jake Fields?"

"A lot of people," he said distractedly, as he flipped another page. "I mean, it wasn't universal, but everyone in Ghost. My agent. My publisher. My writing group. The— Oh my god. This is worse than that drivel you were reading the other day." He jabbed a finger at the book, skewering it with enough phantasmagorical force that the edges jumped. "I *did not* write this."

"Well, you did write the first four and a half chapters, which is all readers would have seen in any online retailer sample. That's one of the reasons your fans were so angry, because it started out like a Jake Fields book—like a Harcourt book—and then practically did a U-turn. One of the great things about

Harcourt was the community he built over the course of the series, and in one book—hell, in one *chapter,* and always off-page—all of them get axed one way or another because he decides they were holding him back and blocking him from seeing what was truly important. After that, stuff just *happens* to him. He has zero agency while he goes on this random journey of self-discovery."

Avi closed his eyes and pinched the bridge of his nose. "Please tell me there wasn't a dream sequence."

"There was a dream sequence." I scratched the back of my head. "Actually, there were eleven."

"Eleven?"

I shrugged apologetically. "What can I say? Harcourt got super into meditation and directed dreaming."

"My editor *hated* dream sequences. She'd never have let this fly. How did my publisher even *get* this?"

"I don't think they did." I rooted around until I found the copyright page. "See? This wasn't published by the same house that handled the other Harcourt books."

Avi's eyebrows snapped down. "Not possible. My agent negotiated an eight-book deal for the Harcourt series with my publisher. A really good deal. We were all happy with it."

"And yet…" I tapped the stack of torn pages. "Here we are." My eyes widened. "Taryn said your will and Oren's were still being contested. I wonder if breach of contract over *Borderline* is one of the reasons."

"For the last time," Avi growled, "there is no such thing as—"

"As *Borderline.* Yeah, I get it. Obviously, some plagiarist SOB self-published this after your death to take advantage of your reputation and the popularity of the Harcourt series." No wonder that other than those first chapters, it was total junk.

Those first chapters.

"Avi, could anyone have found those chapters somewhere online?"

He shook his head. "I deleted them. With extreme prejudice."

"Then the only place they existed was in your trash. In your trash right before you died." I flung out a hand to point at the Lang. "When somebody hit you on the head with a freaking *literary award* and stole your work to pass it off as their own."

"That makes no sense. Just because an author dies, that doesn't mean the killer gets to take over their pen name. And what a stupid thing to do, anyway. It's not like readers can't tell the difference. That kind of deception isn't sustainable."

"I'm guessing the thief figured that out. That's what they're looking for. The real sixth book. If they—" The mass of papers behind Avi began to tremble, and this time they undulated like the surface of a lake at the passing of a huge fish. I gave Avi a stern glare. "Avi."

"Sorry."

"If we..." A sudden glint at the edge of the mess caught my eye. "Hold on a sec."

I pushed myself to my feet and crept closer. There, gleaming on the jewel-toned rug and half-hidden under the open flap of an envelope, was a tiny arc of gold. I picked it up and held it in my palm.

A wedding band.

My heart felt as though it were being squeezed by a vise. As Avi continued to mutter to himself behind me, I teased the envelope out from under the pile. It was blank and unsealed, so I only felt a *little* squicky when I peered inside. Sure enough, it held another, slightly larger gold band, along with some folded papers.

Throat tight, I dropped the ring back in the envelope and pulled out the papers. On top was an itinerary. Two round trip train tickets to Seattle. Vouchers for the ferry from Seattle to Victoria. A reservation at a B & B. A letter from a wedding officiant with a message of congratulations and a confirmation of the time of the ceremony.

The dates were for two days after Avi's death.

At that time, same-sex marriage hadn't been legal in the US, but it was in Canada. Oren had been planning to propose. Instead, he had to mourn.

No wonder he couldn't bear to come back to Ghost.

"A-Avi?"

"Hmmm? God, I can't *believe* how horrible this is."

"I have something to show you, but it might upset you."

"More than somebody putting my name on this absolute *dreck*?"

"Yeah. Pretty sure."

"Fine." The word was laced with long-suffering. "Lay it on me."

I hunkered down and smoothed the itinerary in front of him, then extracted the wedding bands and placed them on top. "I think this was the surprise Oren had for you."

Avi covered his mouth with his hands, but it didn't muffle his sob. A transparent tear dropped toward the paper but left no trace.

"I yelled at him," he said brokenly. "I yelled at him and all the time he had this planned." He touched the smaller band, and both of us sucked in a breath when it moved. With a startled glance at me, he pinched the ring between his thumb and index finger and *picked it up*.

"Holy crap," I whispered.

Avi slid the ring onto the fourth finger of his left hand, where it turned as transparent as the rest of him. Suddenly he was gone—one moment sitting and the next on his feet in the middle of the room.

"Sorry. I'm sorry. But I— I need a minute."

"Sure. Take all the time you need."

After he vanished, I took a breath, rubbing my chest to ease the pinch there. *Damn*. What a thing to hit you on the same day you discover you were murdered and that some asshole stole your last book.

Except...

I stared down at the scatter of torn pages. That wasn't exactly true, was it? *Borderline* wasn't his last book. It wasn't *his* book at all, but there *was* another one. Avi had told me about it. Identity theft. Gaslighting. Undercover at the spa. A mud room scene. The last real last Jake Fields book. *All In*.

And the only person who'd had a copy was Oren.

The way Avi had spoken of it had sounded as though he'd sent Oren a physical copy—something that could potentially be lost during a move—rather than an electronic version.

Well, who just happened to have *all* of Oren's possessions, right here, right now?

"That would be me."

I jumped to my feet and raced for the pantry. If there was half a chance I could do this for Avi—find his last book, maybe turn it in to his agent for posthumous publication to salvage his reputation—then I'd do it.

Even if it meant sorting through every. Freaking. Box.

Chapter Twenty-Nine

Whatever can be said about the people who packed up Oren's effects—and the ability to logically group like articles was not one of them—they were stellar labelers. After playing an intense round of box-Tetris, I hit the mother lode. At the bottom of a stack of six legal-sized banker's boxes was one labeled *Left Nightstand*. Halfway down its list of contents that included *box of tissues, eyeglasses with case, antacids (partial package), phone charger, drafting pencils (3)*, was what I was hoping for:

8-1/2 x 11 spiral-bound book, no cover, approx. 350 pages

That was it. Had to be. Oren was an architect. He wasn't likely to have a lot of other spiral bound books lying around for a little light bedtime reading about electrical codes or building material stress tests, but he was devoted to Avi. I could totally picture him wanting Avi's work close to him.

I briefly considered waiting until Ricky got back so I'd have assistance rearranging the boxes, but I didn't want to wait. Besides, I didn't want Ricky to think I was only interested in him for what he could do for me, such as lugging things up and down stairs, shuttling my cat around, or bringing me dinner.

With silent thanks for Avi's spectral housekeeping talents—the same activities at the Manor had me covered in dust from curls to toes—I rearranged the boxes until I could free my target and lug it out of the pantry.

I set it on the island almost reverently and had just lifted its lid when my phone vibrated in my back pocket. Lid in one hand, I pulled it out to see a text from Ricky:

R: Ok if dinner's delayed by 30?

I shot back a quick *NP* and set the phone aside because there it was, right on top.

All In by Jake Fields.

Just seeing those words on the blue paper cover sheet wasn't what had me clutching the sides of the box, gulping against tears. No, that would be the Post-it fixed to it, right next to the title:

Just a few notes, mostly fanboying. Best thing you've ever written. And I'm not saying that just because I love you. —O

Avi had been worried about Oren's reaction to the book, and I knew from professional experience that even writers as successful as Avi could still suffer from impostor syndrome. Now he'd have validation from the most important person in his life.

I touched the little green square. Would it make Avi feel better or worse? He was already devastated by the news about Oren's proposal plans, about their acrimonious final conversation, so it could go either way.

However, I had no right to gatekeep, for either Avi or Oren, so I left the note where it was, atop the last Jake Fields book.

But… did it *have* to be the last Jake Fields? Avi was still here, after all, and he could use the Smith Corona. Heck, if he wanted to dictate another book, I'd transcribe it for him. Taryn could probably figure out how to handle posthumous publication. Maybe Avi would want to set up a foundation or something with the proceeds. There had to be a way to—

The cell danced on the countertop with another text.

R: Make it 45?

I frowned at the screen. I had no problem waiting, but if something had come up, I didn't want Ricky to feel obligated. I hit the text and called him, putting him on speaker.

"Hey. It's me. Is everything okay?"

"Yeah. My mom sprained her ankle, and—"

"We need to talk about the definition of *okay*, Ricky, because that's not it."

His warm chuckle burred over the line. "She'll be fine. She's already home doing the whole RICE bit. I just have to step in until my cousin can get here to cover her shift."

"Really? Another cousin?"

"What can I tell you? We're everywhere."

"Listen, if you'd rather reschedule—"

"Nah. The good thing about having all these cousins is that there's always one to step into the breach."

"As long as you're sure?"

"Absolutely."

My gaze had remained riveted on *All In* while we talked, and now I reached in and lifted it carefully from its nest of bubble wrap. "You'll never guess what I'm holding right now."

"Uh, Maz? I'm in the middle of restaurant service. This isn't a good time for phone sex."

"What?" I squawked. "No. That's not— We don't— I wouldn't—"

"Relax." He chuckled again. "I know we're not there." His voice dropped. "Yet."

I swallowed a couple of times and refocused. "Yes, well, anyway."

"Tell me. What are you holding right now?"

"I can't actually believe it, but it's here. Oren had it the whole time. The last one. The last book written by the real Jake Fields."

"Jake Fields isn't real."

That sharp comment didn't come from the phone. It came from the family room behind me. I recognized the voice, though, and I probably shouldn't have been as shocked as I was.

I turned slowly, hugging the book to my chest and angling my stance so I blocked the cell's lighted screen. "Carson."

Carson's normally perfect hair flopped to one side, and he was scowling, breathing heavily as if he'd just sprinted for his airport gate, only to miss his flight. "Jake Fields isn't a person. It's a brand."

"You're half right. But putting that aside, I don't recall asking you over. How did you get in?"

"I'm not a vampire. You don't have to invite me before I can cross the threshold." Carson's tone dripped with derision. "The door was unlocked. Besides, I have a key."

"You… have a key."

He rolled his eyes, shaking his head, clearly mistaking my *aha* moment for cluelessness. "Yes, Maz, I have a key. I've always had a key."

Heat built behind my eyes. "So you lied about your access the day we met. Have you been sneaking into the house all along? Ever since Avi died?"

"What? Of course not. I'm not a *criminal*. I'm a *real estate agent*. I *fully* respect property laws. As long as Oren was alive and the legal owner, I waited." Impatience flickered across his face. "Although Avi could have had the decency to leave everything to me in the first place. I *am* his only living relative, and it's not like Oren did anything with it." His expression darkened. "At least not with the *house*. And everything would have reverted to me anyway if they couldn't find Oren's heir."

"I don't think that's true. I'm not an expert on inheritance law, but—"

"No, you're not an expert on anything, are you?"

The scorn in his voice rocked me back on my heels. "Excuse me?" I really hoped Ricky was hearing all this and realized Carson was seriously off the rails.

"I looked you up." He scoffed. "Ghostwriter. What a travesty. You're victimizing real writers."

"Sorry. *What*?"

"You ransom their words."

"I'm not sure where this is coming from, but I provide a service, just like you do with your real estate clients. I work *with* the writers who contract me. There's a dialogue. I assist them in telling their stories so they're ready to move on to editors and proofers."

"Exactly!" His scowl deepened, and he shoved a hand in his blazer pocket. "You take money from them. You shouldn't *charge* them. You should be *grateful for* the privilege of basking in their genius."

I thought about my clients, none of whom were professional writers but who nevertheless had a story to tell. Their work held the promise of being interesting and entertaining, but I'd never describe any of it as *genius*. No writer with real genius needed someone like me.

Then I remembered the conversation with Ricky, about Carson not placing value on professional services that didn't center around something physical, as well as Carson's insinuations about Avi's emotional abuse.

"Carson." I kept my voice as soothing as I could. "Was that the dream you abandoned? The dream to be a writer?"

"I *am* a writer. A *real* one!" Carson's tone was just shy of a shriek. "If Oren hadn't brought that ridiculous nuisance lawsuit, everyone in the world would know by now. I was ecstatic when I heard that he'd died—"

Suddenly Avi appeared behind Carson's shoulder, literal fire in his eyes. "What the *fuck* did he just say?"

"—because I thought it would finally get dropped, but then they found *you* and it all heated up again." He sighed gustily. "If you'd only dated me instead of Ricky, this would have been so much less *inconvenient* for me. However, despite your deplorable lack of taste, I suppose you had your uses." His gaze dropped to the manuscript I was holding up like a breastplate, and he extended the hand that wasn't jammed in his pocket. "Now, if you'd just hand that over, please, we can both get on with our day."

CHAPTER THIRTY

I hugged the manuscript tighter, shaking my head. This might very well be the only copy of Avi's last book. He'd saved his work online, but cloud storage options had been very different ten years ago. Who knew if his accounts were accessible anymore?

Besides, this one had Oren's notes in it, which I suspected would be far more important to Avi now.

"Forget it, Carson. This doesn't belong to you."

"Oh, for the love of—" Carson rolled his eyes. "I'm not going to *publish* it, if that's what you're worried about. I'm going to destroy it."

"What?" I croaked. "Why?"

"Because it's unnecessary. The brand has moved on." He glanced over his shoulder at the family room fireplace. "If it makes you feel better to witness it, we can burn it right here."

I backed up until the counter pressed into my lower back. "Absolutely not. It's got Oren's notes in it."

Avi's gaze snapped to me, and the rage on his face morphed into desperate hope. "Really?"

I nodded. "On the cover and in the text."

"So what?" Carson said. "His scribblings can't be important to you. You'd never even met the man. You said so yourself."

Avi flashed away from Carson's side and appeared next to me. "Show me?"

I tipped the manuscript forward enough that he could see the Post-it on the cover, and he raised trembling hands to his mouth.

"It doesn't matter that I'd never met him, Carson. He was still part of my family, and I intend to respect his wishes."

Carson's eyes narrowed. "Well, I'm Avi's family. What about his wishes?"

"Pretty sure those were laid out in his will," I said dryly. "He leave anything to you? Anything at all?"

"Obviously, Avi would have wanted things to go to Oren when he was alive. I can grant that they were devoted to one another. But Oren's dead." Next to me, Avi twitched at Carson's dismissive tone. "I'm sure Avi would want anything that was his personal property to go to *his* family, not some random stranger."

"Is that right?" I drawled.

"In a pig's eye," Avi muttered.

"Of course." Carson's breathing had evened out, and he'd recaptured the self-assurance he wore like his two-hundred dollar shirt. "And clearly, as the last of his family, I'm the best curator of his legacy."

Avi scoffed. "I wouldn't trust him to curate the contents of my refrigerator."

I couldn't help it. I laughed, which brought a thundering scowl to Carson's face, as though I'd actually offended him. "What are you laughing about?"

"I'm pretty sure the job description of a literary curator doesn't include burning an author's final manuscript."

"I told you. The brand has moved on. Readers wouldn't want an obviously inferior product."

Okay, call me oblivious, but it wasn't until that moment that the shoe finally dropped. From the audible intake of Avi's breath, he got it, too.

"It was you," we both said.

"What was me?" Carson said.

"You published *Borderline*."

Carson huffed an irritated sigh. "No. *Jake Fields* published *Borderline*."

"You know perfectly well that Jake Fields is Avi's pen name. The Harcourt series is his intellectual property. You had no right to pretend to be him."

"I didn't pretend to be anybody. Jake Fields isn't a real person. It's a *brand*. *Borderline* is my fresh Jake Fields rebrand."

"You can't do that. While author names aren't always unique, their story worlds coupled with their names are protected."

Carson waved a hand in front of his face as though swatting away an insect. "That's why I waited to publish until the full seven was up, even though it only took me five to write the book."

"That dreck took him five years?" Avi said, at the same time that I said, "Full seven what?"

"Years, you moron. *Years*. You know, the length of time you have to wait before somebody is declared dead?"

I rubbed my eyes with one hand while not easing my hold on *All In* with the other. "Carson, there was no question over whether Avi was alive. He died in full view of most of the town. There was a body. A funeral."

"I'm not talking about *Avi*. I'm talking about *Jake Fields*."

"Yes, so am I. You understand how copyright works, don't you?"

Carson's face resembled Gil's when I tried to foist a healthier cat food option on him—an equal mix of confusion, mistrust, and outrage. "What are you talking about?"

"Copyright protection lasts for the author's lifetime plus seventy years, or, for pseudonymous works, the earlier of ninety-five years from first publication or 120 years from creation. Avi wrote those first few chapters of *Borderline*, and the only way you could have included them is if you stole them out of his wastebasket."

"I didn't *steal* them. He'd thrown them away."

"Pretty sure removing something from a house without his permission counts as stealing, regardless of where the item is located. In any case, a writer's work is copyrighted as soon as it's on the page, whether that page is physical or electronic, published or not." I jerked my chin at him. "Since you have your own key, I'm guessing you walked in on Avi when he was working, didn't you?"

"I knocked. He didn't answer."

"I was wearing noise-canceling headphones," Avi said. "Trying to focus."

"So you barged in anyway?" I couldn't keep the edge out of my voice. I *really* hoped Ricky was still on the line, but I didn't want to risk checking behind me to make sure. "And then you coshed him on the head with a freaking *literary award*?"

"It's not like he *deserved* that award." Carson matched my rising volume. "He was a *hack*. His books weren't *real* literature."

"Yet people bought his books. Loved them. Begged for more."

"All the more reason for him to help me educate readers on what *real* literature truly is. I gave him everything he needed. The character names. The setting. The plot. I did all the work for him. He didn't have to do anything but use my creativity and inspiration to write the book."

"Oh, my god." Avi slapped his forehead. "Is he still on about that? Nobody wants to read about a self-righteous house flipper spouting pop philosophy between tedious descriptions of dry rot."

I glanced at him sidelong. "Hate to tell you, but…"

He stared at me, clearly aghast. "You don't mean—Harcourt?" When I nodded, he said, "If I wasn't already dead, I'd ask you to just kill me now."

I snorted and Carson scowled again. "What do you hate to tell me?"

"You realize you're describing my job, right?" Since Carson believed that I should provide my services for free for the privilege of basking in my clients' glorious words, I guessed he'd expected the same thing from Avi. "Ghostwriting requires a certain skill set and mindset. Avi didn't vet other people's manuscripts. He wrote his own."

"He could have *helped*. He *owed* me those chapters. He threw them away, but *I* took them from there. *Borderline* was the new Jake Fields. A better Jake Fields. Readers won't want an inferior retro brand when they've got the new one to look forward to. So you see"—he jammed his right hand into his pocket, and I really didn't like how that pocket seemed to bulge with more than a fist—"that manuscript is irrelevant. You might as well hand it over now."

"Do you think he has a gun in his pocket?" I murmured to Avi.

"Pretty sure," Avi replied.

"Why are you talking about me in the third person?" Carson barked. "I'm *right here*."

He pulled his hand out of his pocket, and yep. Gun.

I kept very still. "Anything you can do with that?"

My question was directed at Avi, although since I kept my attention focused on Carson, he, of course, assumed I was talking about him.

"I can do *plenty*." He waved the gun around. From the way it was shaking, I seriously doubted his ability to aim, but who knew whether that would be a benefit or a drawback? "I *practice*. You can do anything if you *practice*. That's all Jake had to do. Help me practice, but he *never* took me seriously. I wrote him dozens of letters, but he never responded."

"Wait." I shot another glance at Avi, but he wasn't there. *Great. No backup.* I *really* hoped Ricky was listening. "You wrote letters to Jake Fields?"

Carson sneered at me. "Of course I did."

"You realize that you could have just talked to him, right?"

He blinked. "I can't talk to him. He isn't real."

My head was starting to ache, probably from the adrenaline buzzing through my veins because a guy who was obviously divorced from reality was aiming a gun in my general direction. "When did you write all these letters?"

"What do you mean?"

"The letters to Jake Fields. When did you write them?"

"After the lawyers made all the retailers stop selling *Borderline*. I had to prove it. Prove there could be no response, no *permission*, because Jake Fields wasn't real. Once I'd proved it, then they'd have to put the book back on sale and I could get my money."

Money. It was always about money, sex, power, or revenge, wasn't it? At least, that's what my retired detective client claimed in his book.

"Carson," I said softly but firmly, wondering where Avi had gotten to and hoping like hell that if Ricky *was* in Avengers-assemble mode, that he wouldn't appear and startle Carson into taking a wild shot. "Jake Fields was Avi's pen name. He couldn't have answered those letters because he was already dead."

Although I mentally tagged *Since you killed him* onto that sentence, I didn't say it out loud, because, you know, gun. Carson was clearly unbalanced at the moment and I didn't trust him not to take the giant step from blunt force trauma to GSW.

"Exactly. Proof, just like I said. Then I proved that anyone could be Jake Fields because he *isn't real*. He's a brand just like Carolyn Keene. Betty Crocker. Mark Twain. *Brands*, not people."

He waved the gun again. It was a revolver, I could tell that much, but the eye of the barrel looked odd. As I watched, a dribble of sawdust drifted from the gun's nose to the floor.

Avi.

Would the gun still fire if the barrel was stuffed with sawdust? Even if it did, I doubted it would do Carson's aim any favors. Maybe it would jam. Might it explode in his hand? I didn't know. But I expect Carson wouldn't know either.

In any case, I wanted to give Avi plenty of time, so despite the danger that I might set Carson off, I decided to keep him talking.

"Carolyn Keene was the work-for-hire pseudonym the Stratemeyer Syndicate used for the ghostwriters who produced the Nancy Drew books, just like they used Laura Lee Hope for the Bobbsey Twins and Victor Appleton for Tom Swift. Betty Crocker started as a fictional character created to respond to customer queries before General Mills turned her into a brand."

"See?" Carson crowed. "I told you. Not a real person. A *brand*."

I inclined my head. "In that case, yes. But a trademark-protected brand. Mark Twain, on the other hand, was the pen name for the very real Samuel Clemens. Just because somebody writes pseudonymously doesn't mean that person isn't real."

The gun barrel was totally packed with sawdust by this time, and beneath the beat of my heart in my ears, I caught the telltale creak of the front door easing open. At least I *hoped* it was the door, although Carson didn't appear to register the sound.

"Look, I know you didn't intend to kill Avi. But if you shoot me, that's pretty intentional, don't you think?"

Carson pressed his trembling lips together, although he didn't lower the gun. In fact, he pointed it straight at me. "I didn't mean to kill him. I just wanted him to *help*. It's not like it would have cost him anything to *help*."

"You didn't just want him to *help*. You wanted him to write the book *for* you, and that would have cost his time, and his time had a real, significant value because he used it to earn his own living." I hugged the manuscript closer, mentally crossing my fingers. "The other thing about trying to shoot me? If you try to fire that gun, things might not turn out the way you plan. When's the last time you maintained it?"

He barked a laugh. "Nice try. I cleaned it this morning."

"Yeah? What did you use? Garden mulch? Because it looks like the barrel is full of sawdust."

"What?"

He turned the gun toward himself, his mouth dropping open when he saw the blocked barrel, just as a tall, broad-shouldered woman who looked like she could be *my* cousin hustled into the room behind him with Ricky at her back.

Chapter Thirty-One

The deputy—I assumed that's who it was, since she had the khaki uniform, the badge, and a gun holstered on her belt—grasped Carson's wrist and forced his arm to his side with no apparent effort.

"Carson," she said, her voice calm and kind. I realized if she was stationed in Ghost, she probably knew all the locals personally. "Why don't you give that to me? You don't want to do anything you'd regret, now, do you?"

"I have a right to protect myself, Kamilla."

"That's as may be, but accosting an unarmed man in his own home is not a good look for you." She nodded at Ricky, who stepped forward and held out an evidence bag.

He quirked a smile at me as she dropped the gun inside. "I'm a volunteer reserve deputy."

"Of course you are." I laughed weakly. My knees buckled and I ass-planted on the tile, my back to the island, as the deputy cuffed Carson and led him away. "One of these days, you'll need to tell me what your actual job is."

"It's a date." He held up the bag. "I have to accompany Kamilla back to her patrol car, but once Carson's secured, I'll be back. Are you all right?"

"I'm… recovering."

"Good. Hold that thought."

He disappeared down the hall and I heard the front door close. The next instant, Avi reappeared and collapsed next to me. Evidently ghostly legs could get wobbly as much as physical ones.

He braced his elbows on his knees and dropped his head into his hands. "I can't believe Carson attacked me."

"Avi." I let my head thunk back against the island. "He *killed* you. He may not have intended to, but he hit you in the head, knocked you out, stole your work, and didn't even bother to check back to see if you were okay. If he'd gotten you medical attention right away, you might have been fine."

His shoulders lifted and he mirrored my head thunk, although his was silent. "Or maybe not. There's no way to tell." He winced. "I have to admit, I could have been nicer to him about his literary aspirations. If he needed a writing coach—"

"He so did," I muttered. I'd read *Borderline,* unable to reconcile *that* Jake Fields with the Jake Fields who knew how to keep readers on the edge of their seats, turning pages and not counting the cost of sleepless nights.

"Regardless, I would have been the wrong choice. I'm not—or rather I wasn't—known for my patience. Or tact, for that matter."

"I'm not sure anybody would have been right. I mean, I like to think I'm good at my job, but I have my limits, and I try to keep them in mind when I evaluate a prospective project. If a concept or manuscript is beyond my skill level, it wouldn't be fair to the client or me to take the job. I couldn't have saved *Borderline* with the literary equivalent of an IV, a heart transplant, and an iron lung." I smiled at him. "Nice work with the sawdust, by the way. Where did that come from?" I hadn't seen any in the spotless basement.

Avi shrugged. "Same place the dust goes, I guess." He smiled back at me. "If I ever figure it out, I'll let you know."

There was a brisk knock at the front door, followed by Ricky's voice. "Maz? It's me. Okay if I come in?"

"We're in the kitchen," I called. "Come on back."

The door closed softly and Ricky's footsteps padded along the hardwood floor before he peeked into the kitchen, Gil's carrier in his hand. He scanned the room and his eyebrows lifted. "We?"

I gestured to my ghost housemate. "Avi."

Ricky nodded toward Avi. "Hola, Avi." He set the carrier down and opened its door. "Sorry if you weren't ready for Gil's homecoming, but Tia's hosting her scrapbooking group tonight, and he… forgot himself among the embellishments."

"I should have named him Magpie. He can never resist shiny things."

I held out my hand and Gil bounded out. Instead of heading for me, though, he trotted over to Avi, looked up at his face, and mewed.

Avi shared a wide-eyed glance with me as Gil stepped over Avi's crossed ankles as though they were perfectly visible and settled into the cradle made by his legs. Avi lifted a tentative hand and stroked along Gil's spine. He looked up at me, smile filled with wonder. "I can feel his fur. It's so soft."

Indeed, Gil's ginger fur lifted behind Avi's hand, just as it did when I petted him on especially dry days.

"He likes you." I chuckled and scratched behind Gil's ears. "I've always said he's a better judge of character than I am." I looked up at Ricky. "Avi foiled Carson's attack with sawdust until you could get here with the cavalry. Impeccable timing, by the way. Thank you." I glanced back at Avi, whose attention was still focused on Gil. "Thank you both. You'll always be heroes in my book."

"Ah. Well. Sure." Ricky looked away and scratched the back of his head. "So, are you hungry? You probably don't want to go out for dinner right now, but I can run over to the taqueria and get some takeout."

I couldn't help the sigh that escaped me, because I really didn't want to leave the house. In fact, I might not be able to move from this spot in the foreseeable future.

Like I said. Hero.

"That would be wonderful."

His smile was still edged with that adorable bashfulness. "Trust me on the menu options?"

"Absolutely."

"Excellent. I won't let you down." He raised a hand in Avi's direction and then headed down the hall.

"He's a really nice guy. Always was, even as a kid." Avi's words were nearly drowned by Gil's purr. "You picked a good one."

"Yeah," I sighed again, and this time I sounded more like a moony teenager. "I'm lucky he's willing to give me a chance."

Avi snorted a laugh. "You have no idea, Maz."

I frowned at him. "What's that supposed to mean?"

"Nothing, nothing." He waved a hand, earning him a bat of Gil's paw, which… didn't pass right through him.

Huh. Too bad Gil couldn't talk, because he seemed to have a better handle on this ghost business than either of us. Clearly we needed to test Avi's… powers? Abilities? Phantasmagorical talents? I sensed a montage opportunity in our future.

When I realized I was still holding *All In,* I figured this might be a good start. I set it on the floor in front of him. "Can you pick this up?"

He stared down at the manuscript, biting his lip. "I'm almost afraid to try." But he reached out anyway. Unfortunately, his hand passed through it without even budging the Post-it. "Guess not."

"Hmmm." So much for my theory that he could hold things that belonged to him, like his own wedding band, but not Oren's. Gil didn't belong to him, but do cats ever belong to anybody? "Try manipulating the individual pages, the way you did in the library with the deconstructed *Borderline.* That might be harder to do with the spiral binding, but I can cut that off if it would make things easier."

He cut me a startled glance, but then his jaw firmed and his eyes took on a determined glint.

At first, nothing happened. Then the corner of the blue cover quivered. The next instant, it whipped to the side, the top third tearing away from the binding. I whooped, but he just laughed a little breathlessly.

"Clearly I lack finesse."

"Sure, but this is great! I bet with a little practice, you can nail it. Look at your control over sawdust." I gazed down at the title page. *All In by Jake Fields*. "Your fans are going to go ballistic when they find out there's a last *real* Harcourt and Corchran book."

Avi's hand stilled on Gil's back and he gazed at me, expression troubled. "I don't understand, Maz. Why didn't Oren turn the book in to my agent? She could have handled everything with the publisher. The deal for the TV rights hadn't been finalized either because it was contingent on this book."

"I think I know." I stroked between Gil's ears in the place he liked best. "It was his last link to you. His last chance to hear your voice."

"But he missed out on all those royalties." Horror filled his eyes. "Oh god. The publisher's advance. Since I didn't deliver the book, he'd have had to pay it back."

Maybe that's why Oren's estate was asset rich but cash poor. I decided not to lay that on Avi right now.

"I suspect the money didn't matter to him." I met Avi's gaze. "You know where I found it? In a box labeled *Left Nightstand*. He kept it there, at his bedside, where he could reach out and touch it in the dark. Keeping you close. Even after all those years."

Tears glittered in Avi's eyes and he sucked in a sharp breath before turning away. "I yelled at him, Maz," he said, voice hoarse. "Almost the last time we talked, I accused him of not prioritizing our relationship."

"But he did." I cursed the fact I couldn't at least pat Avi's shoulder. "And your last words to him weren't angry, remember? They were a promise. You promised you'd wait, and you kept that promise."

"And he promised that he'd prove that I was wrong, that he'd show me our relationship was the most important thing—that *I* was the most important thing in the world to him." Avi glanced down at *All In* and then held out his left hand, where the wedding band glowed in transparent gold. "He kept that promise, didn't he?"

"I'd say so, yeah. Big time."

Avi met my gaze, eyes bright with hope. "Would you… That is, would it bother you if I stuck around? He also promised he'd come back, so if I keep waiting, maybe he'll make good on that promise, too."

"Wait as long as you want." I smiled, and although his return smile was a little watery, it was still sweet. "We like the company."

Gil, always one to get the last word, mewed.

Dear Reader,

Thank you so much for reading *Ghostridden*, the first in Ghost Townies, my small town supernatural cozy mystery series. I'm so happy you've taken this journey with me! I'd be immensely grateful if you'd take a moment to leave a review at the retailer and any other site you use for reviews. Believe me, reviews make an *enormous* difference to the health and well-being of books (and not incidentally, to their associated authors!).

Pop on over to my website, https://ejrussell.com, for all the deets on my books—my paranormal rom-coms and mysteries, my contemporary romances, and my one lone historical. If you're an audio fan, you can find the audio scoop there too. (The QR code on the next page will get you there with your smartphone camera or other code reader.)

Would you like exclusive content and ARC giveaways, not to mention gratuitous dance videos? Then I'd love for you to join me in E.J. Russell's Reality Optional, my Facebook fan group (https://facebook.com/groups/reality.optional). My newsletter is the place to get the latest dish on new releases, sales, and more. I promise I only send one out when I've got…well…news. You can subscribe here: https://ejrussell.com/newsletter.

All my best,

—E

Paranormal Romance
Mythmatched Universe
Fae Out of Water Trilogy
Cutie and the Beast
The Druid Next Door
Bad Boy's Bard

Supernatural Selection Trilogy
Single White Incubus
Vampire With Benefits
Demon on the Down-Low

Other Mythmatched Romances
Howling on Hold
Possession in Session
Witch Under Wraps
Cursed is the Worst
The Skinny on Djinni
Assassin by Accident (part of Carnival of Mysteries)

Quest Investigations Mysteries
Five Dead Herrings
The Hound of the Burgervilles
The Lady Under the Lake
Death on Denial

At Odds with the Gods (A Mythmatched / Purgatory Playhouse crossover)

Mythmatchedlets (Mythmatched companion stories, free to newsletter subscribers in ebook form, collected in one paperback volume: *Second First Date, Rusty's Really Bad Day, First Flight, Getting the Band Together, Purgatory Postscript, A Very Quest Solstice*)

Magic Emporium Series (shared world)
Purgatory Playhouse

Enchanted Occasions Series
Best Beast
Nudging Fate
Devouring Flame

Ghost Townies Series
Ghostridden

Legend Tripping Series
Stumptown Spirits
Wolf's Clothing

Art Medium Series
The Artist's Touch
Tested in Fire
Art Medium: The Complete Collection (omnibus edition)

Royal Powers Series (shared world)
Duking It Out
Duke the Hall
King's Ex

Science Fiction
Sun, Moon, and Stars Series
Partnership
Principles

Interdimensional Time Bureau
Monster Till Midnight

Historical Romance
Silent Sin

Contemporary Romance
Camera Shy
Summer Kitchen
The Thomas Flair
Mystic Man
For a Good Time, Call… (A Bluewater Bay novel, with Anne Tenino)

Christmas Kisses (holiday shorts)
The Probability of Mistletoe
An Everyday Hero
A Swants Soiree

Geeklandia Series
The Boyfriend Algorithm (M/F)
Clickbait

Writing as Nelle Heran
(traditional cozy mystery)

Crafty Sleuth Series (with C.K. Eastland)
Die Cut
Mixed Media
Found Objects (*coming soon)*

About the Author

E.J. Russell (she/her), author of the award-winning Mythmatched paranormal romance series, writes LGBTQ+ romance and mystery in a rainbow of flavors. Count on high snark, low angst, and happy endings.

Reality? Eh, not so much.

She's married to Curmudgeonly Husband, a man who cares even less about sports than she does. Luckily, C.H. also loves to cook, or all three of their children (Lovely Daughter and Darling Sons A and B) would have survived on nothing but Cheerios, beef jerky, and Satsuma mandarins (the extent of E.J.'s culinary skill set).

E.J. also writes traditional cozy mystery as Nelle Heran. She lives in rural Oregon, enjoys visits from her wonderful adult children, and indulges in good books, red wine, and the occasional hyperbole.

News & Social Media:
Website: https://ejrussell.com
Newsletter: https://ejrussell.com/newsletter

Acknowledgements

I owe many thanks to my long-suffering editor, Meg DesCamp; to my Darling Son B, Nicholas Katen, for agreeing to be my cover model; to Sam San Román for photographing him so beautifully; to L.C. Chase for the groovy cover; to lyric apted for beta reading; to NOLAKim, PA extraordinaire, for support (and making sure I'm not a *total* recluse); to the Crit Posse (L.C. Chase, Amy Aislin, and Lee Blair) for cheerleading and reality checks; to my family, who puts up with my eccentricities with only occasional eyerolls.

And, always and forever, thank you to my readers for accompanying me on this journey. You're the reason I can continue to follow my heart, and I appreciate you more than I can say.

www.ingramcontent.com/pod-product-compliance
Lightning Source LLC
Chambersburg PA
CBHW031227260626
47169CB00007B/2189

* 9 7 8 1 9 4 7 0 3 3 9 9 3 *